REVENGE

Story by
Brian Smith

Art by
Erwin Prasetya
Angga Prasetyawan
Alfa Robbi

SACRIFICE

Story by
Cory Levine

Art by
Maurizio Campidelli

MONSUNO: COMBAT CHAOS
Volume 2
REVENGE/SACRIFICE

REVENGE
Story by Brian Smith
Art by Erwin Prasetya, Angga Prasetyawan & Alfa Robbi
Inks by Arum Setiadi & Fandhi Gilang Wijanarko
Colors by Fajar Buana
Letters & Additional Colors by Zack Turner

SACRIFICE
Story by Cory Levine
Art by Maurizio Campidelli
Letters by Zack Turner

Design/Sam Elzway
Editor/Joel Enos

Printed in China

Published by VIZ Media, LLC
P.O. Box 77010
San Francisco, CA 94107

10 9 8 7 6 5 4 3 2 1
First printing, September 2013

vizkids
www.vizkids.com

RATED A FOR ALL AGES
PARENTAL ADVISORY
MONSUNO is rated A and is suitable for readers of all ages.

VIZ media

VOLUME 2
REVENGE/SACRIFICE

TABLE OF CONTENTS

CHARACTERS

CHASE & LOCK

Chase is on a quest to both find his missing father, the scientist who discovered Monsuno, and figure out a way for humans and Monsuno to coexist peacefully. He's learning how to be the hero that he needs to be to make that happen. Chase's Monsuno, the powerful and loyal Lock, was left for him by his father.

BREN & QUICKFORCE

Chase's best friend since childhood. He is a fast-talking genius, but he lacks courage. Bren's loyal Monsuno is the volatile Quickforce.

JINJA & CHARGER

The unpredictable Jinja has no patience for bad guys. She's quick to act and even quicker to tell you if you're wrong! Her Monsuno is the tough-skinned Charger.

BEYAL & GLOWBLADE

Beyal is a mystic monk who would rather meditate than fight. He has a strong spiritual connection to Monsuno that none of his friends have yet developed. Beyal's Monsuno, Glowblade, is a scorpion-like reptile that is always ready to strike at its master's command.

DAX & AIRSWITCH

Dax is the rebel of the team. His act-first-think-later attitude sometimes gets him and his clawed Monsuno, Airswitch, into trouble.

DR. KLIPSE

The main villain in the Monsuno story. He wants to co
the world by demolishing society and creating a new
order where he rules with the power of Monsuno
Monsuno of choice is the terribly scary Backslash.

DR. MOTO

Her secret
experiments with
Monsuno are about to
get out of hand...way
out of hand!

HARGRA

Dr. Klipse's lo
butler is full o
creepy secre

THE STORY OF
MONSUNO

65 MILLION YEARS AGO – Meteors fell to Earth carrying
life-forms made out of powerful, chaotic, uncontrollable
genetic material. This was the Monsuno—origin unknown
and the real reason why the dinosaurs became extinct!
Soon after, the Monsuno essence fell dormant and
stayed that way for millions of years...until...

TODAY – A potent energy source is discovered in the
K-layers of the planet. Scientist Jeredy Suno believes
he's found a solution to the ever-mounting energy crisis.
But what he doesn't know is that this green energy
source is a ticking time bomb!

When Dr. Suno goes missing, his 15-year-old son, Chase,
ventures out to find him. Chase discovers the power of
Monsuno, and now he and his friends are in an all-out race
for survival against dangerous villains seeking power
and a secret government agency seeking control of the
most powerful creatures ever known...the Monsuno!

Chase and the rest of Team Core-Tech have traveled to
the mysterious underground lab of Dr. Moto, where she
has been conducting experiments to create and control
new mutant Monsunos. While there, one of Dr. Moto's
colleagues, Dr. Hurtz, betrays Dr. Moto, trapping Team
Core-Tech with the mutant Monsunos in the underground

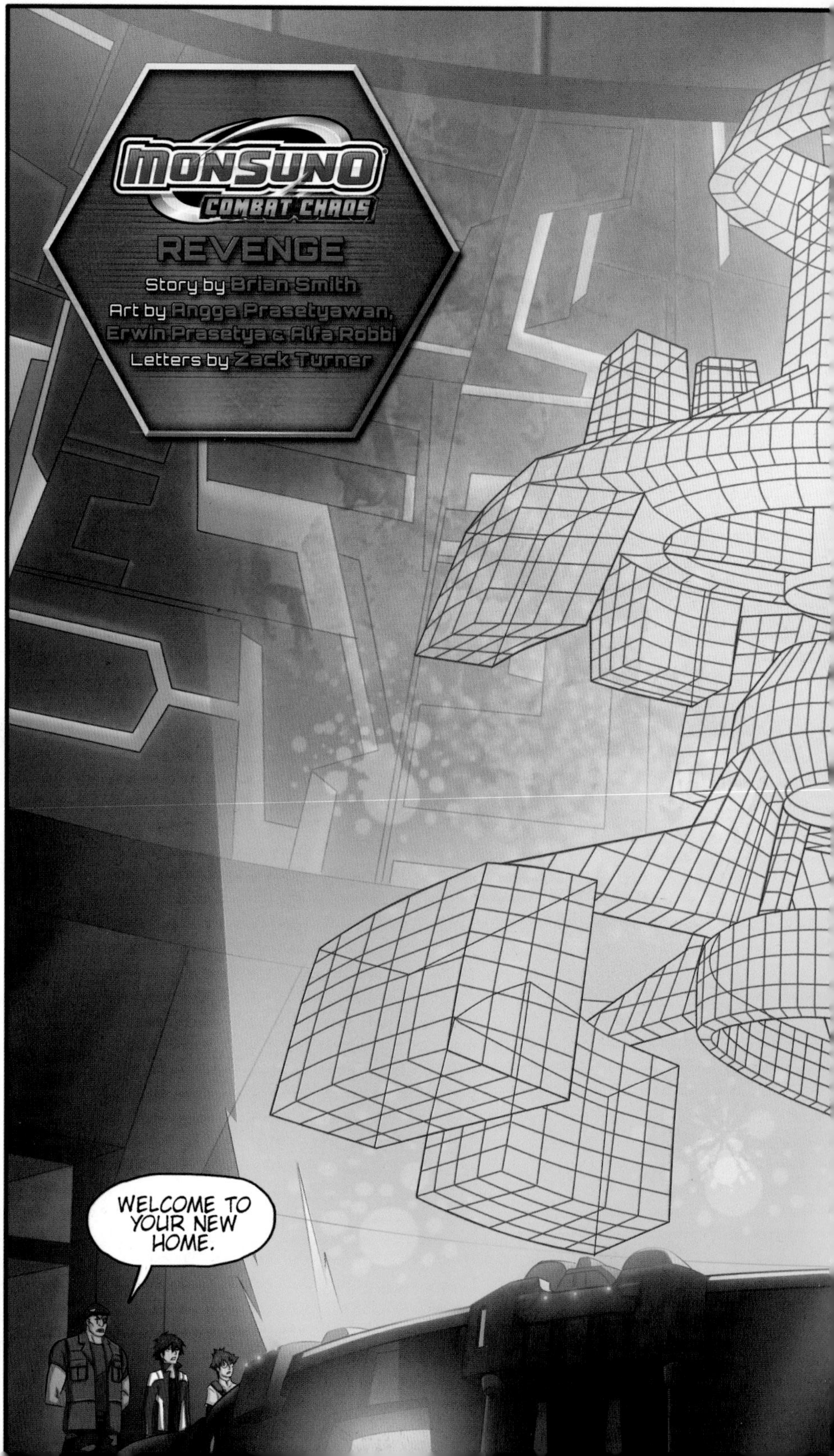
MONSUNO
COMBAT CHAOS
REVENGE
Story by Brian Smith
Art by Angga Prasetyawan, Erwin Prasetya & Alfa Robbi
Letters by Zack Turner
WELCOME TO YOUR NEW HOME.

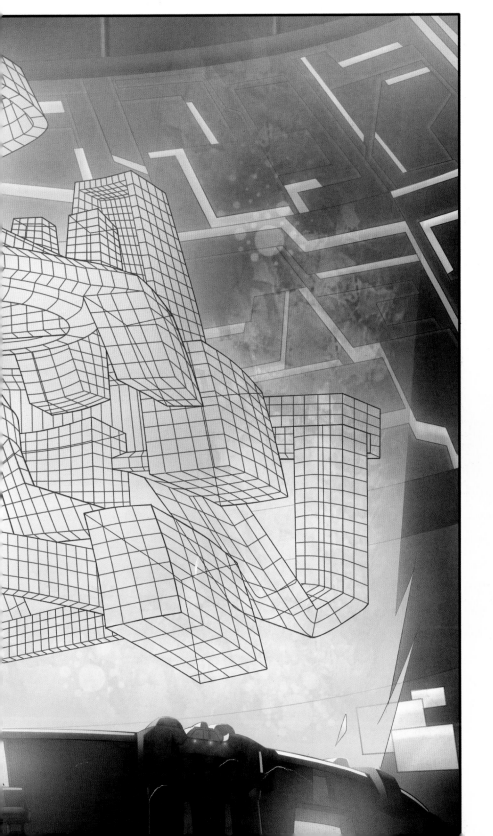

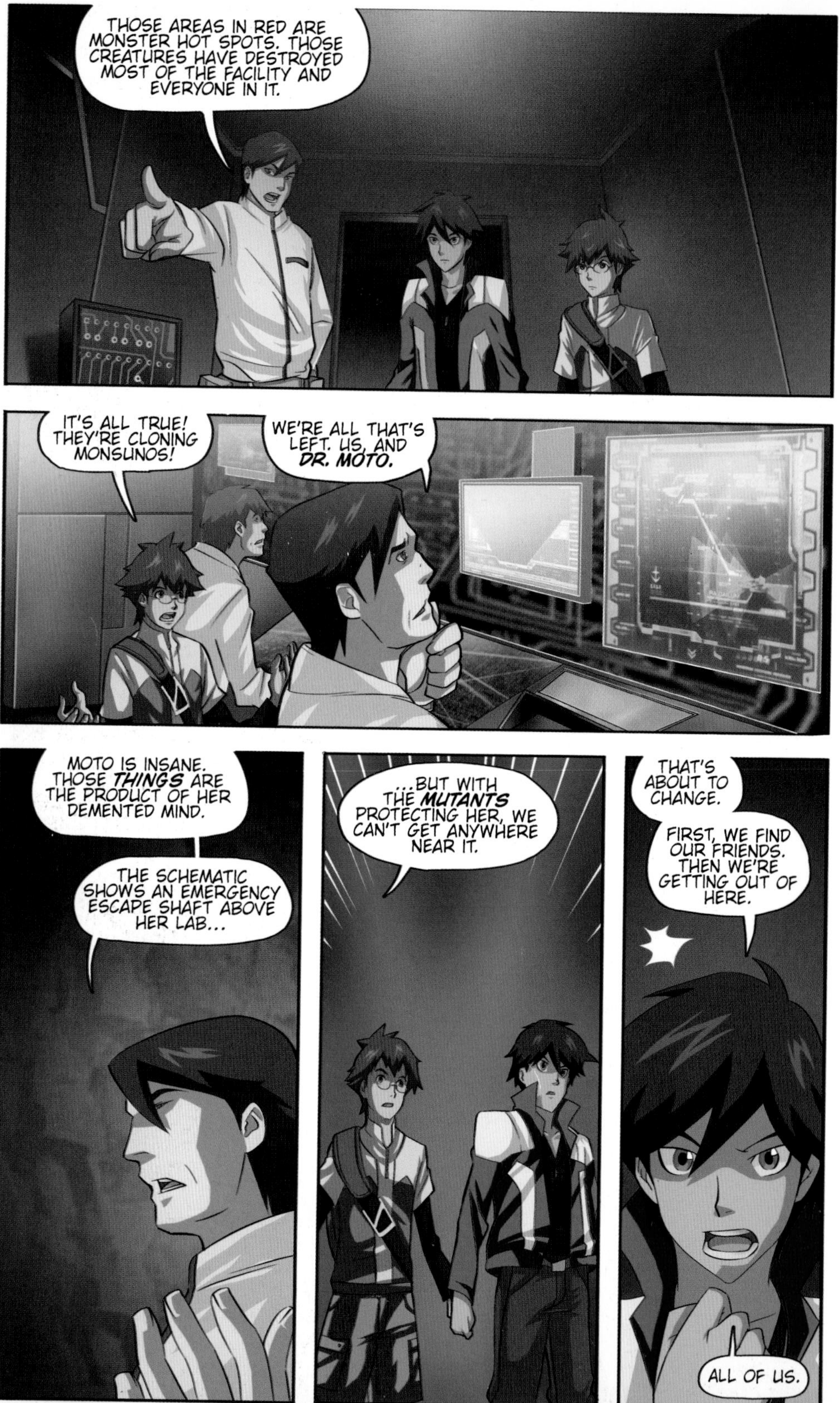
THOSE AREAS IN RED ARE MONSTER HOT SPOTS. THOSE CREATURES HAVE DESTROYED MOST OF THE FACILITY AND EVERYONE IN IT.
IT'S ALL TRUE! THEY'RE CLONING MONSUNOS!
WE'RE ALL THAT'S LEFT. US, AND DR. MOTO.
MOTO IS INSANE. THOSE THINGS ARE THE PRODUCT OF HER DEMENTED MIND.
THE SCHEMATIC SHOWS AN EMERGENCY ESCAPE SHAFT ABOVE HER LAB...
...BUT WITH THE MUTANTS PROTECTING HER, WE CAN'T GET ANYWHERE NEAR IT.
THAT'S ABOUT TO CHANGE.
FIRST, WE FIND OUR FRIENDS. THEN WE'RE GETTING OUT OF HERE.
ALL OF US.

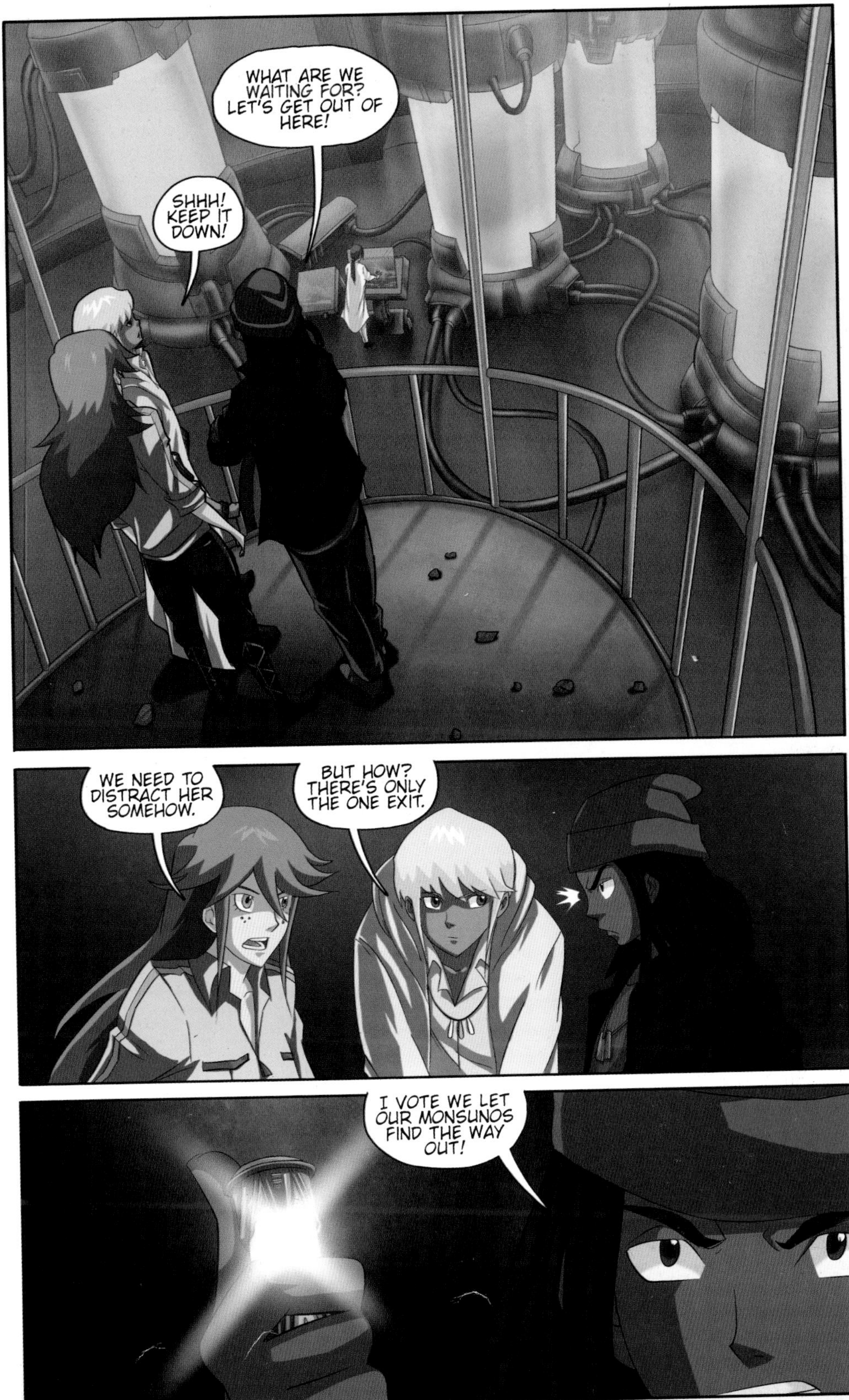
WHAT ARE WE WAITING FOR? LET'S GET OUT OF HERE!
SHHH! KEEP IT DOWN!
WE NEED TO DISTRACT HER SOMEHOW.
BUT HOW? THERE'S ONLY THE ONE EXIT.
I VOTE WE LET OUR MONSUNOS FIND THE WAY OUT!

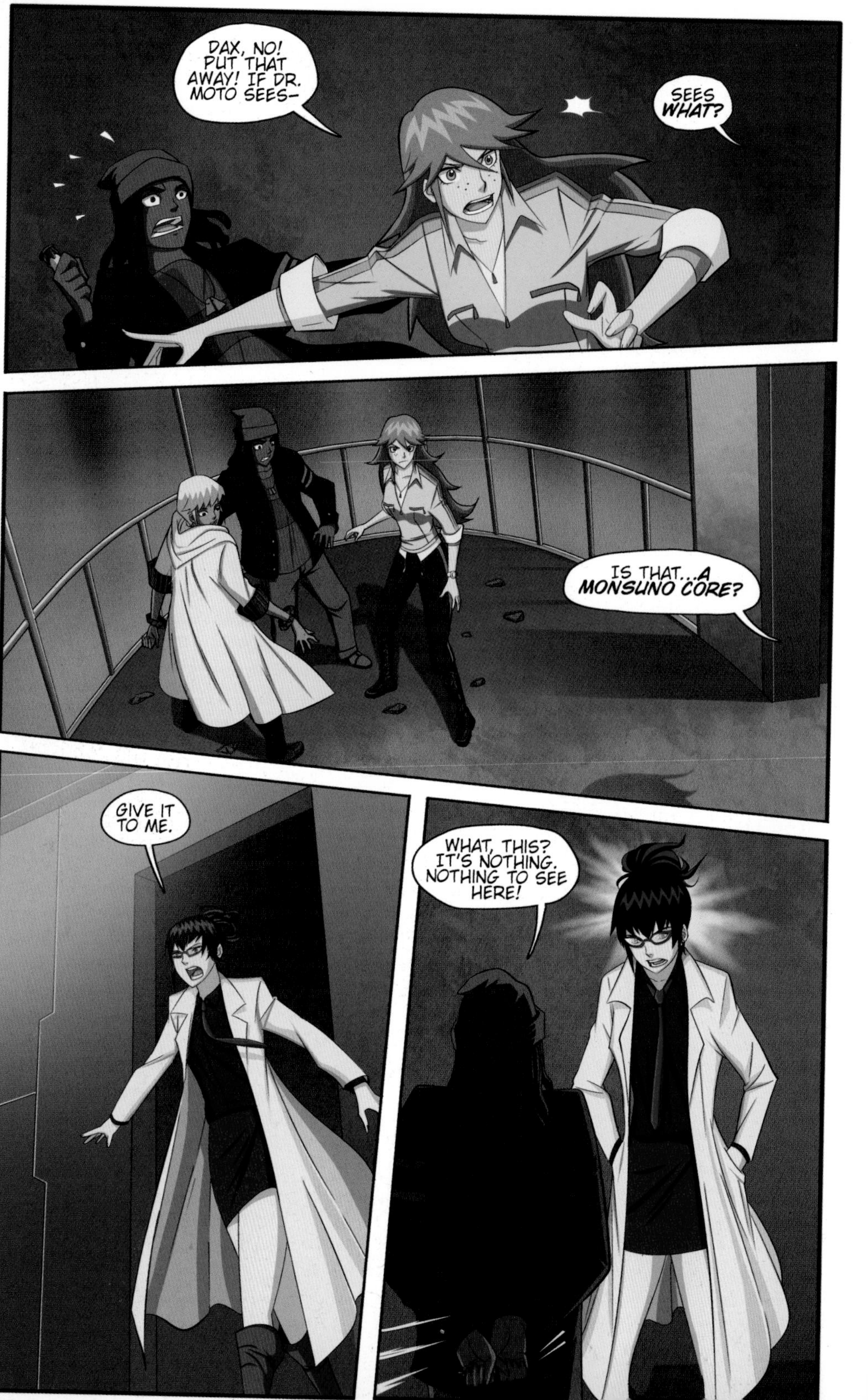
DAX, NO! PUT THAT AWAY! IF DR. MOTO SEES—
SEES WHAT?
IS THAT...A MONSUNO CORE?
GIVE IT TO ME.
WHAT, THIS? IT'S NOTHING. NOTHING TO SEE HERE!

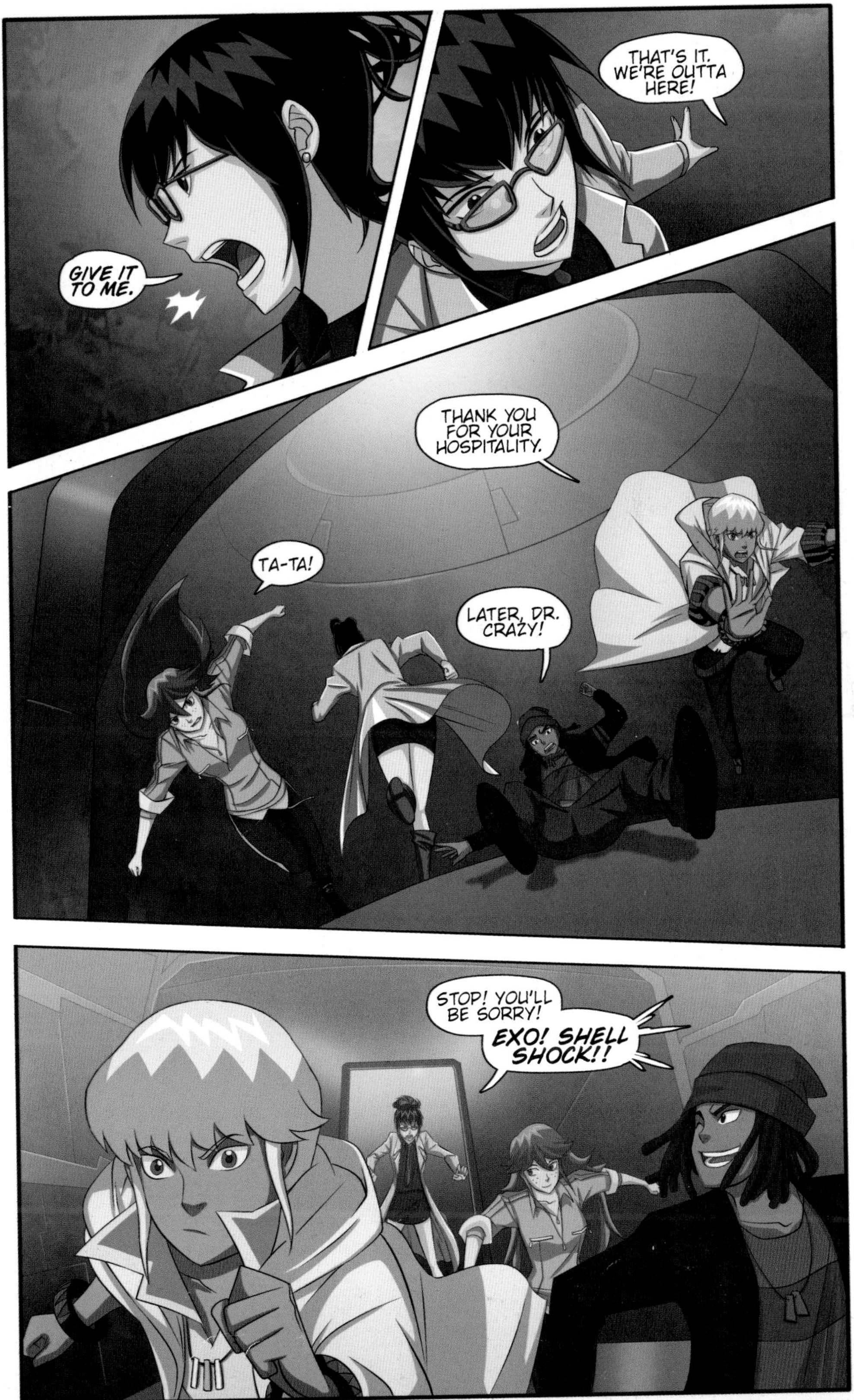
GIVE IT TO ME.
THAT'S IT. WE'RE OUTTA HERE!
THANK YOU FOR YOUR HOSPITALITY.
TA-TA!
LATER, DR. CRAZY!
STOP! YOU'LL BE SORRY!
EXO! SHELL SHOCK!!

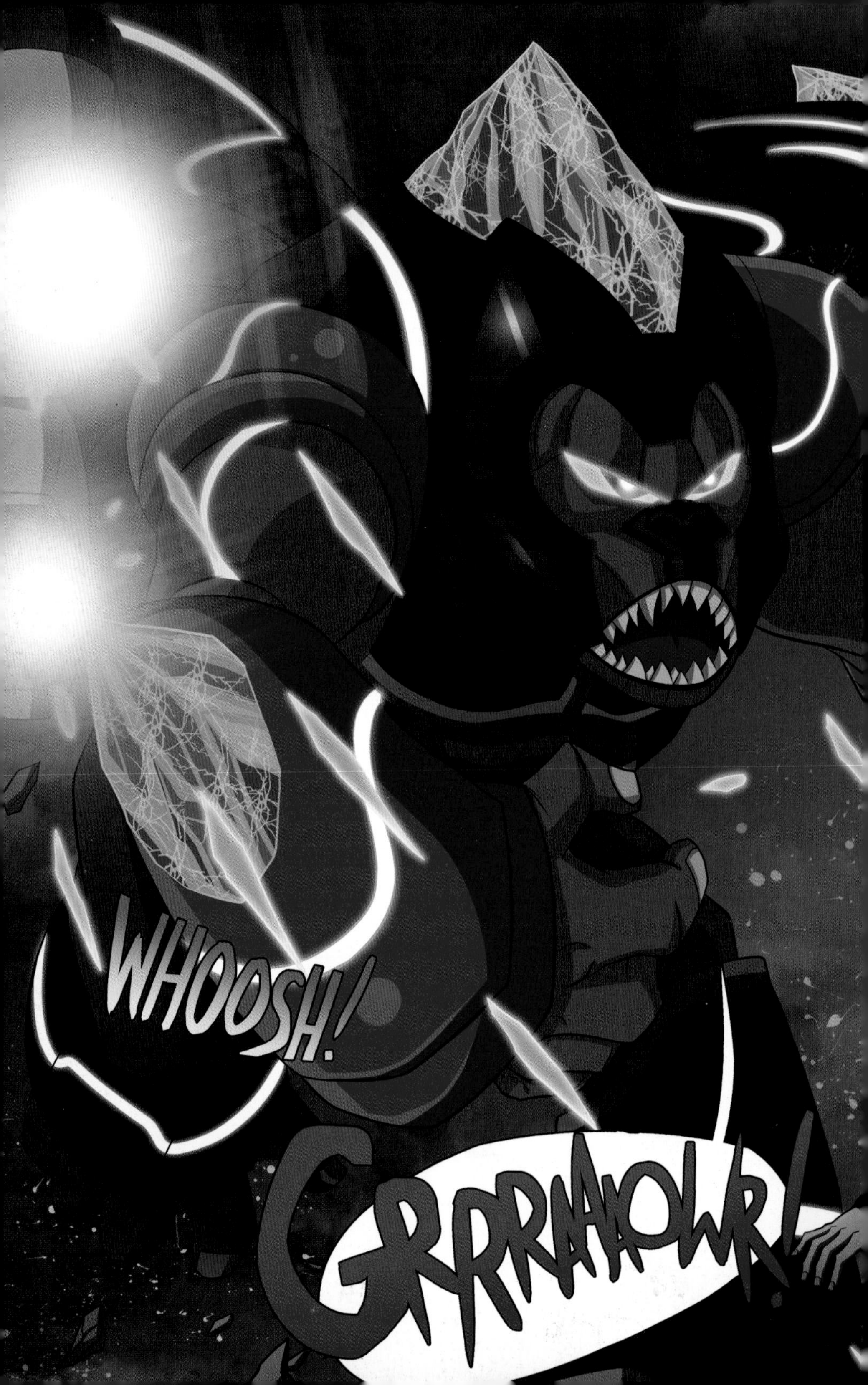
WHOOSH!
GRRRAAOWR!

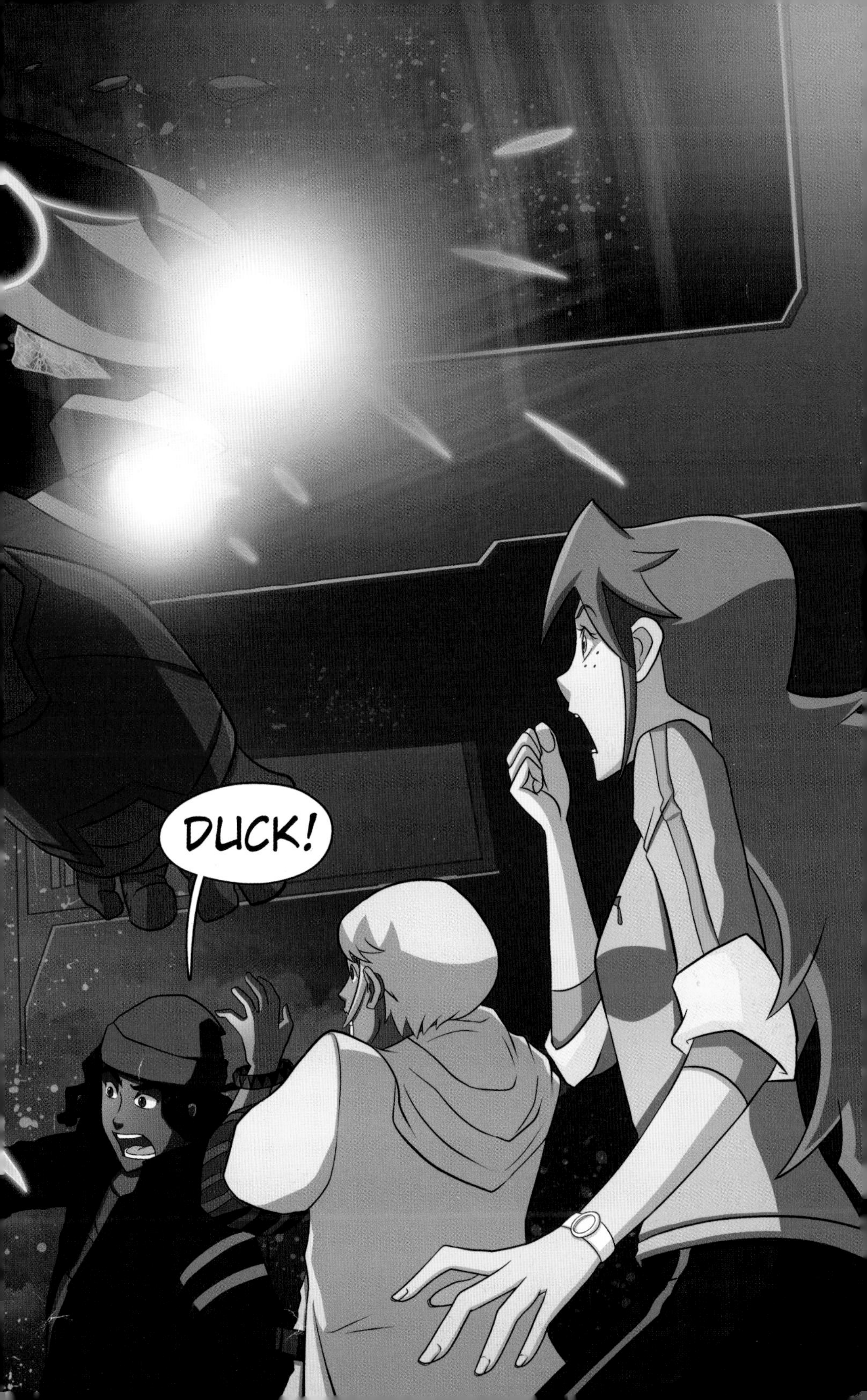
DUCK!

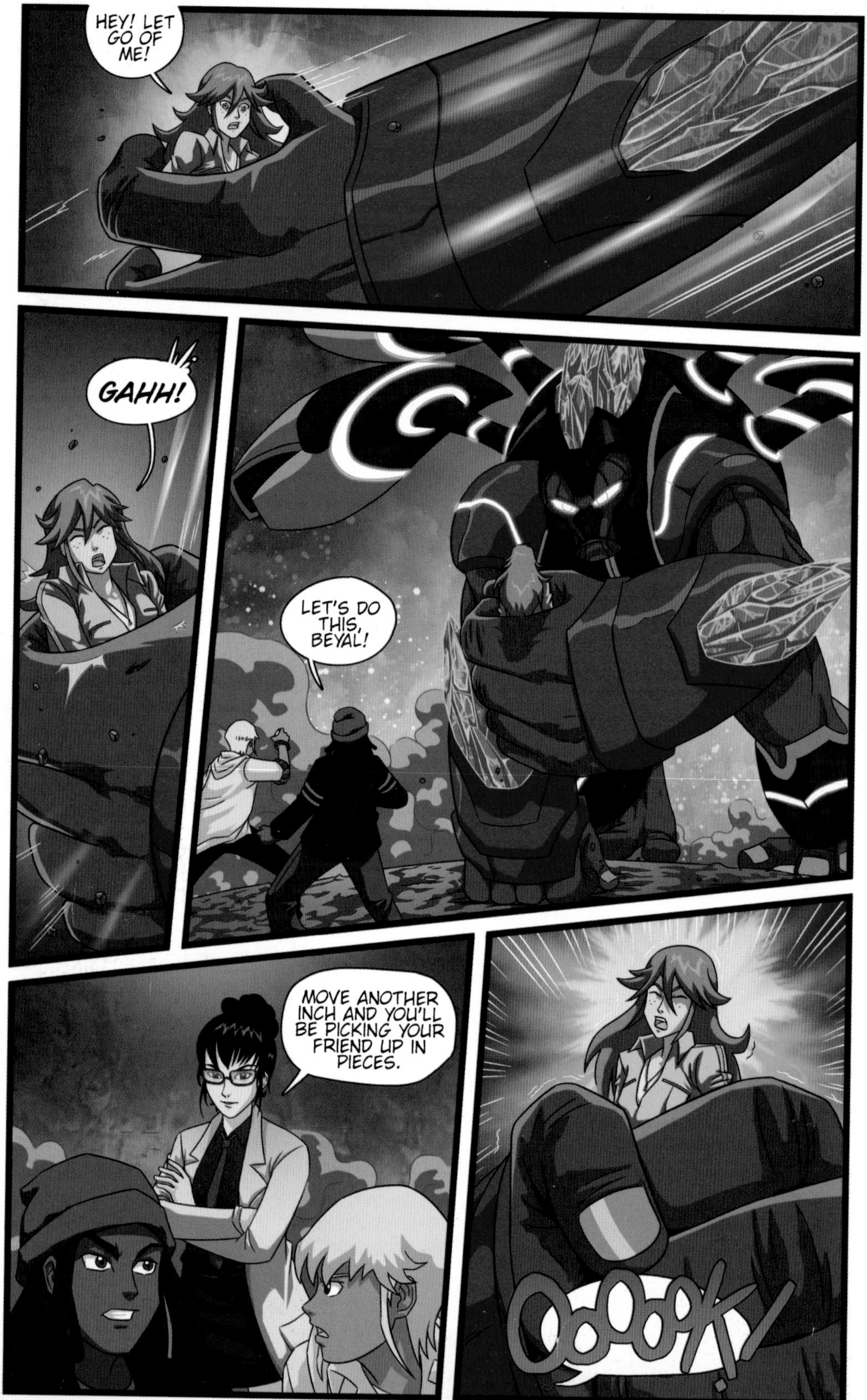
HEY! LET GO OF ME!
GAHH!
LET'S DO THIS, BEYAL!
MOVE ANOTHER INCH AND YOU'LL BE PICKING YOUR FRIEND UP IN PIECES.
OOOOOK!

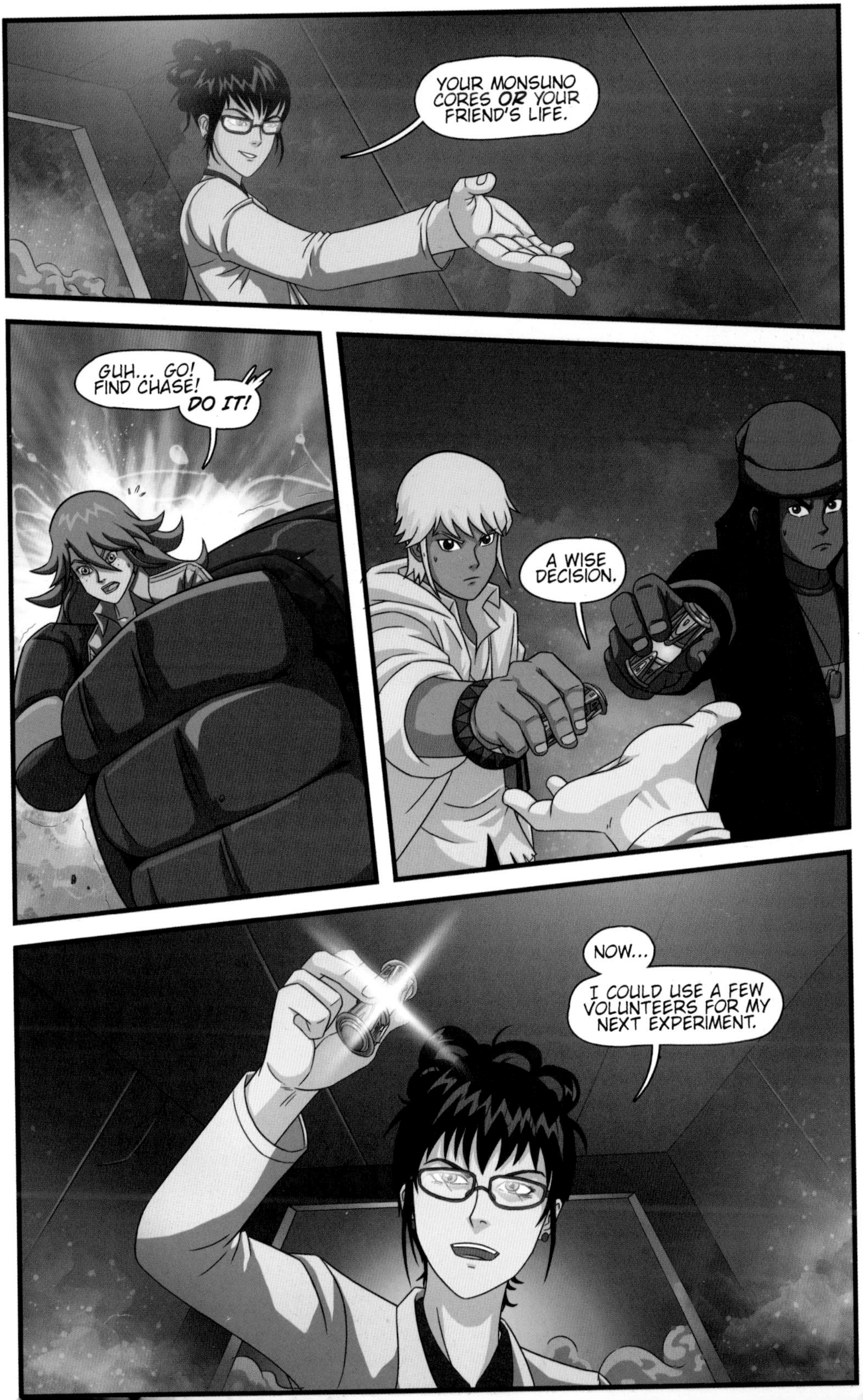
YOUR MONSUNO CORES **OR** YOUR FRIEND'S LIFE.
GUH... GO! FIND CHASE!
DO IT!
A WISE DECISION.
NOW...
I COULD USE A FEW VOLUNTEERS FOR MY NEXT EXPERIMENT.

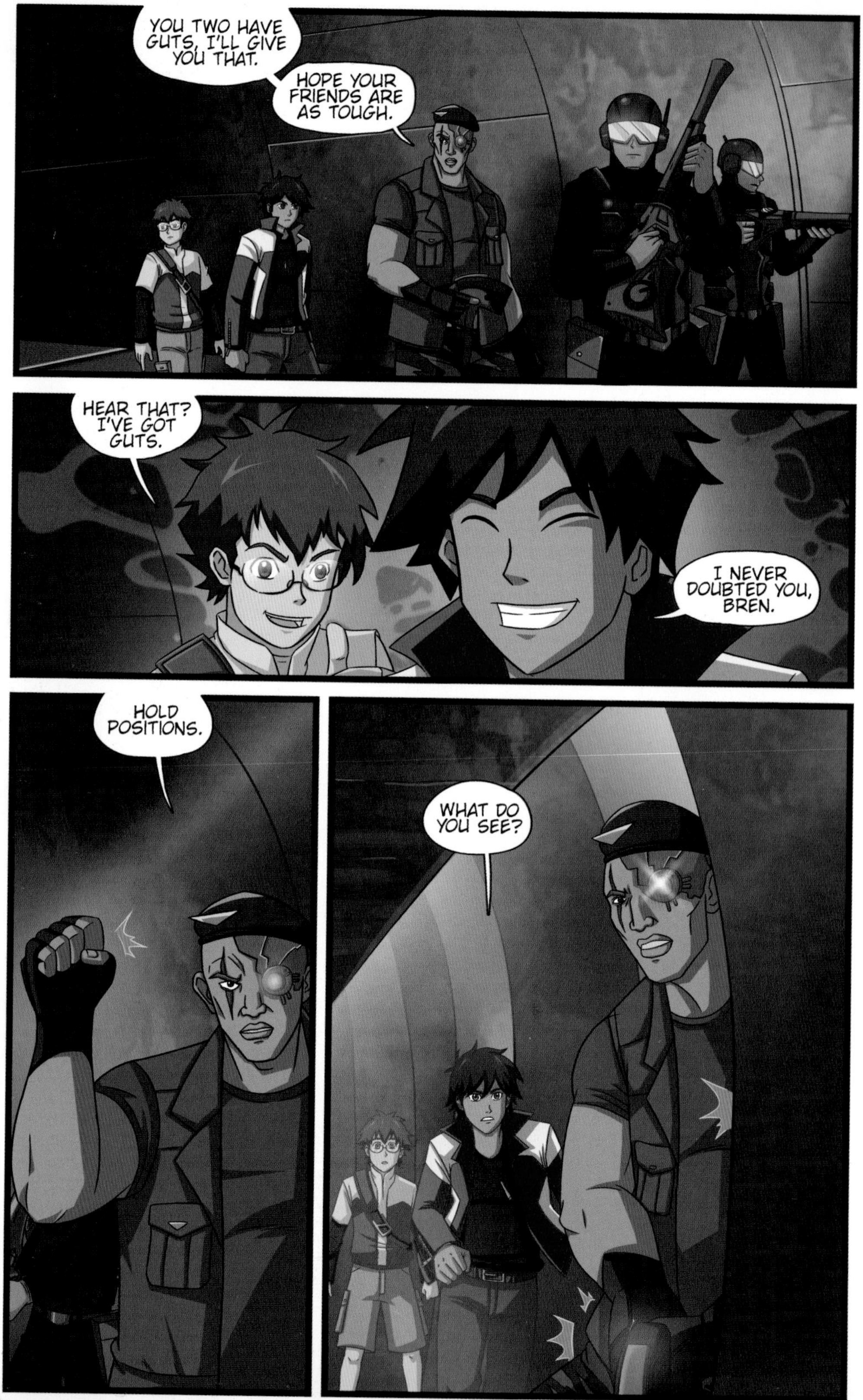
YOU TWO HAVE GUTS, I'LL GIVE YOU THAT.
HOPE YOUR FRIENDS ARE AS TOUGH.
HEAR THAT? I'VE GOT GUTS.
I NEVER DOUBTED YOU, BREN.
HOLD POSITIONS.
WHAT DO YOU SEE?

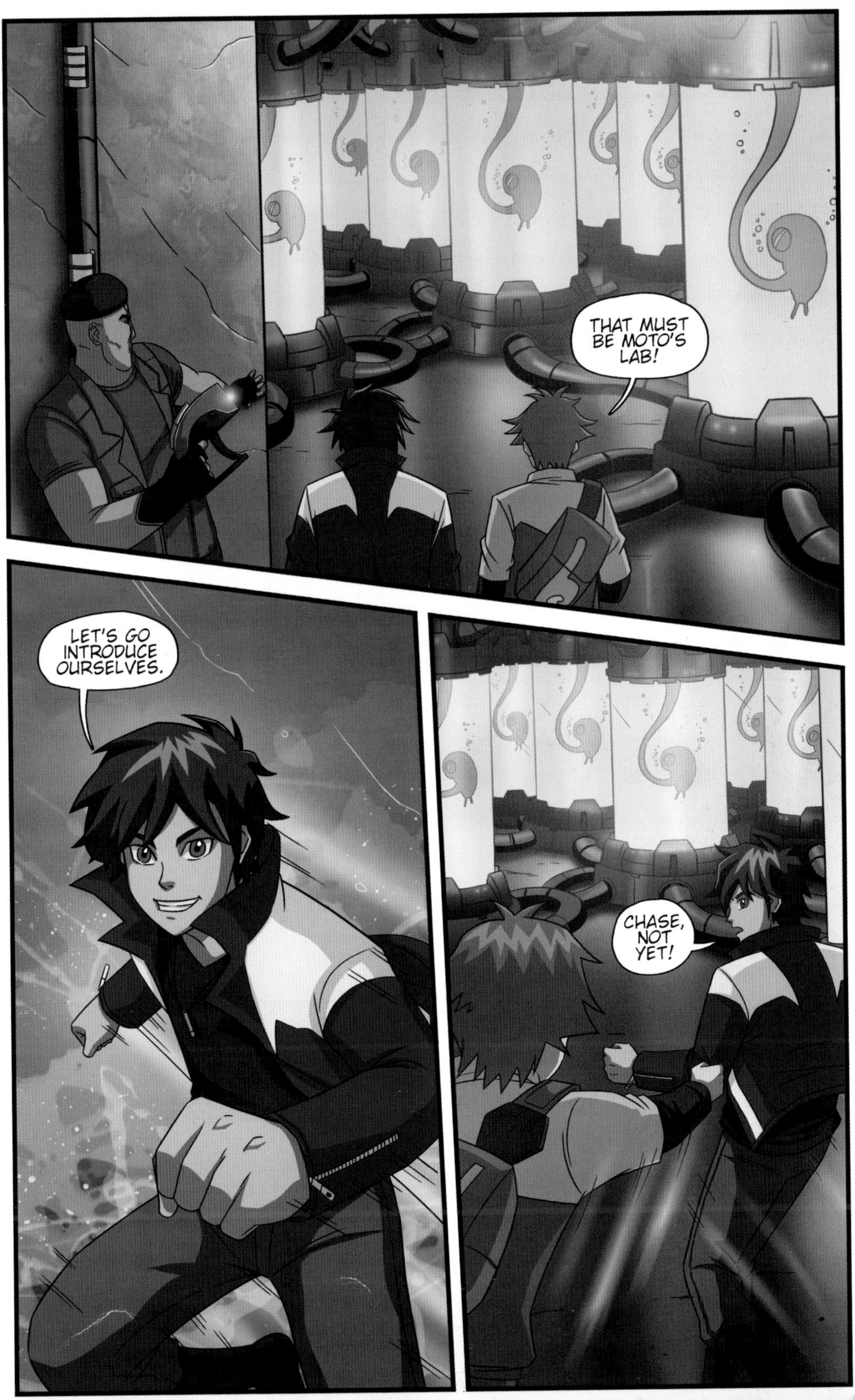
THAT MUST BE MOTO'S LAB!
LET'S GO INTRODUCE OURSELVES.
CHASE, NOT YET!

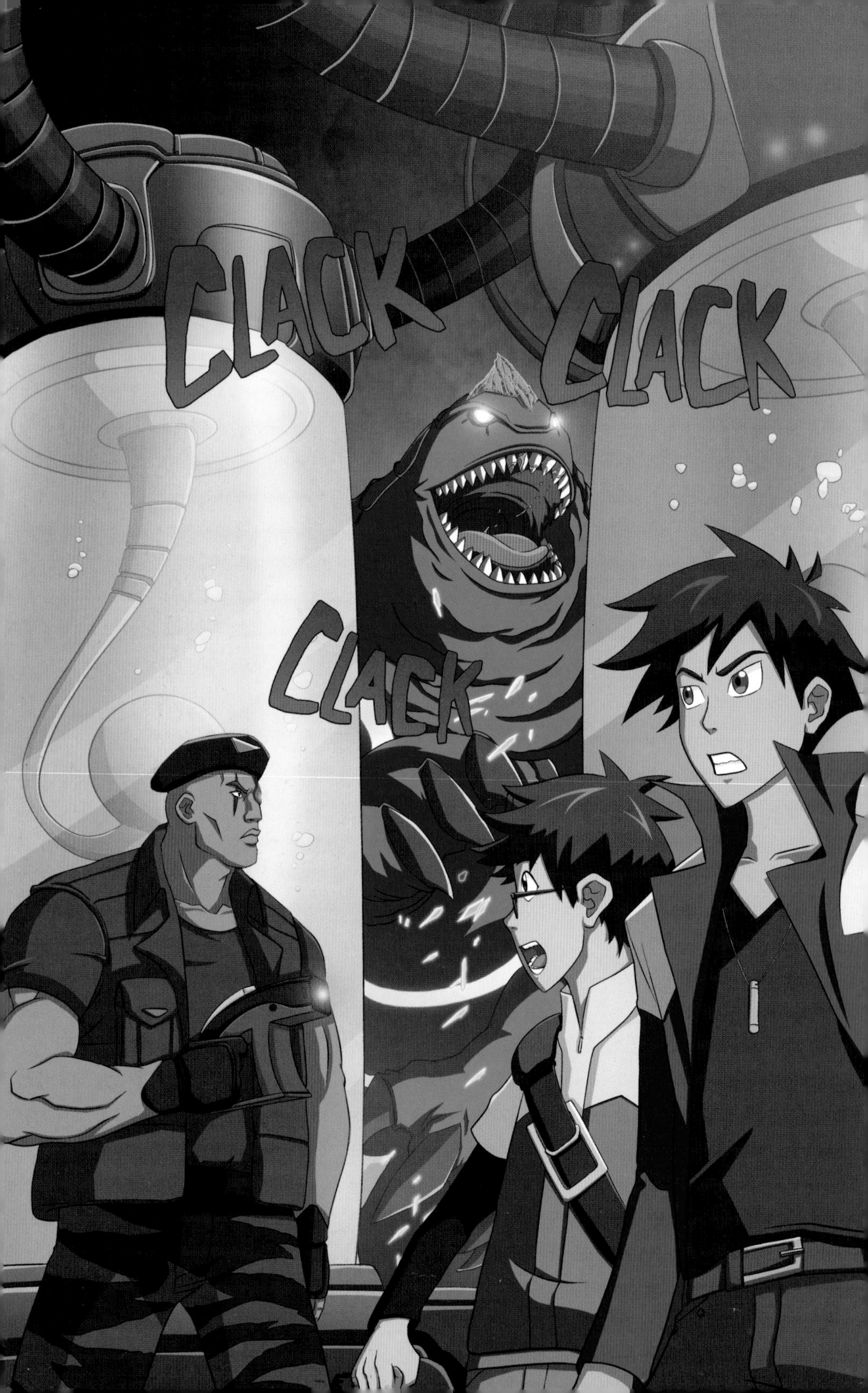
CLACK
CLACK
CLACK

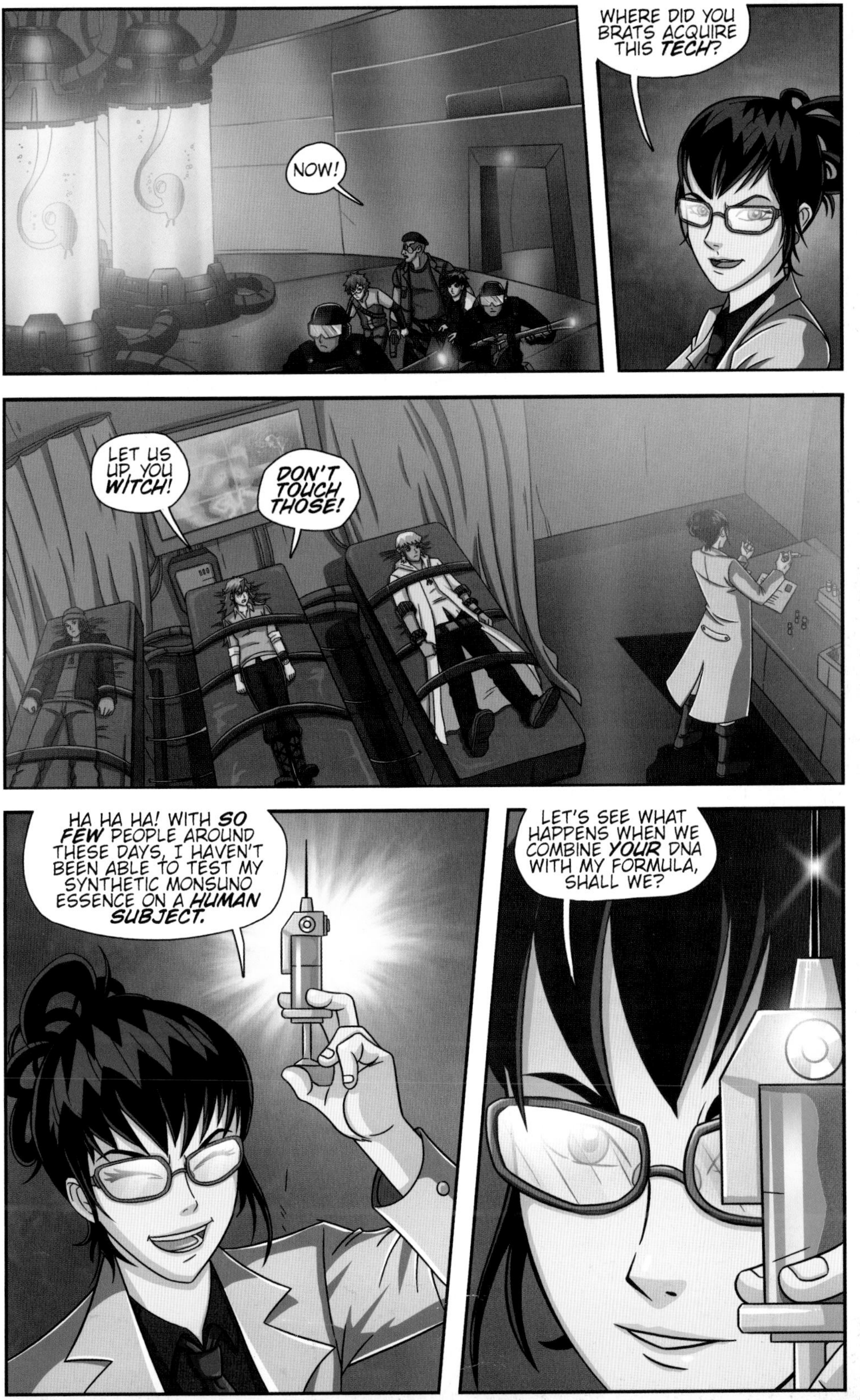
NOW!
WHERE DID YOU BRATS ACQUIRE THIS TECH?
LET US UP, YOU WITCH!
DON'T TOUCH THOSE!
HA HA HA! WITH SO FEW PEOPLE AROUND THESE DAYS, I HAVEN'T BEEN ABLE TO TEST MY SYNTHETIC MONSUNO ESSENCE ON A HUMAN SUBJECT.
LET'S SEE WHAT HAPPENS WHEN WE COMBINE YOUR DNA WITH MY FORMULA, SHALL WE?

JINJA, DAX, BEYAL...

WE'RE COMING, GUYS.

WHAT DO YOU THINK? WE CAN SNEAK AROUND BACK, SURROUND HER...

I'M SORRY, BOYS.

SORRY? FOR *WHAT*?

THIS.

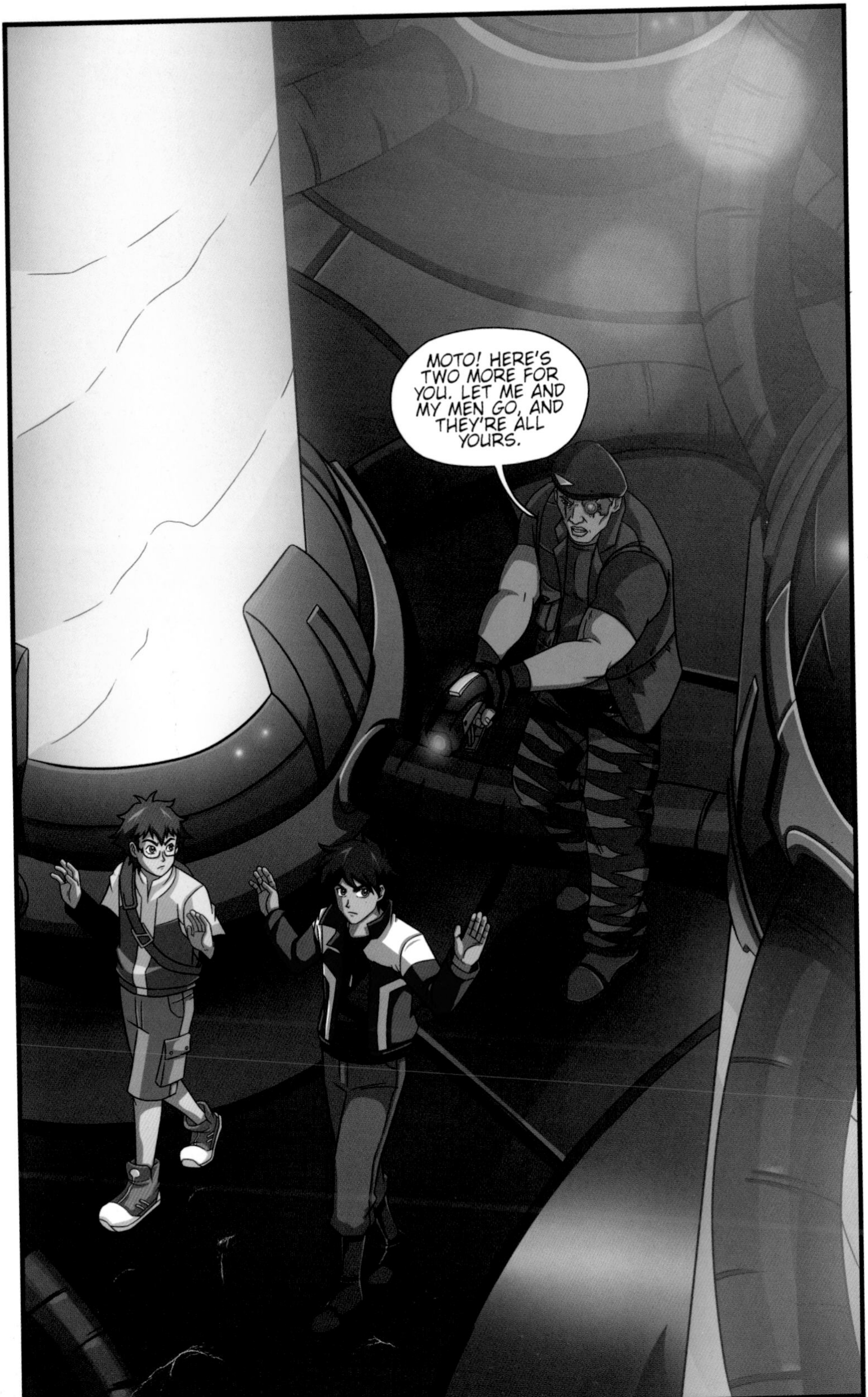
MOTO! HERE'S TWO MORE FOR YOU. LET ME AND MY MEN GO, AND THEY'RE ALL YOURS.

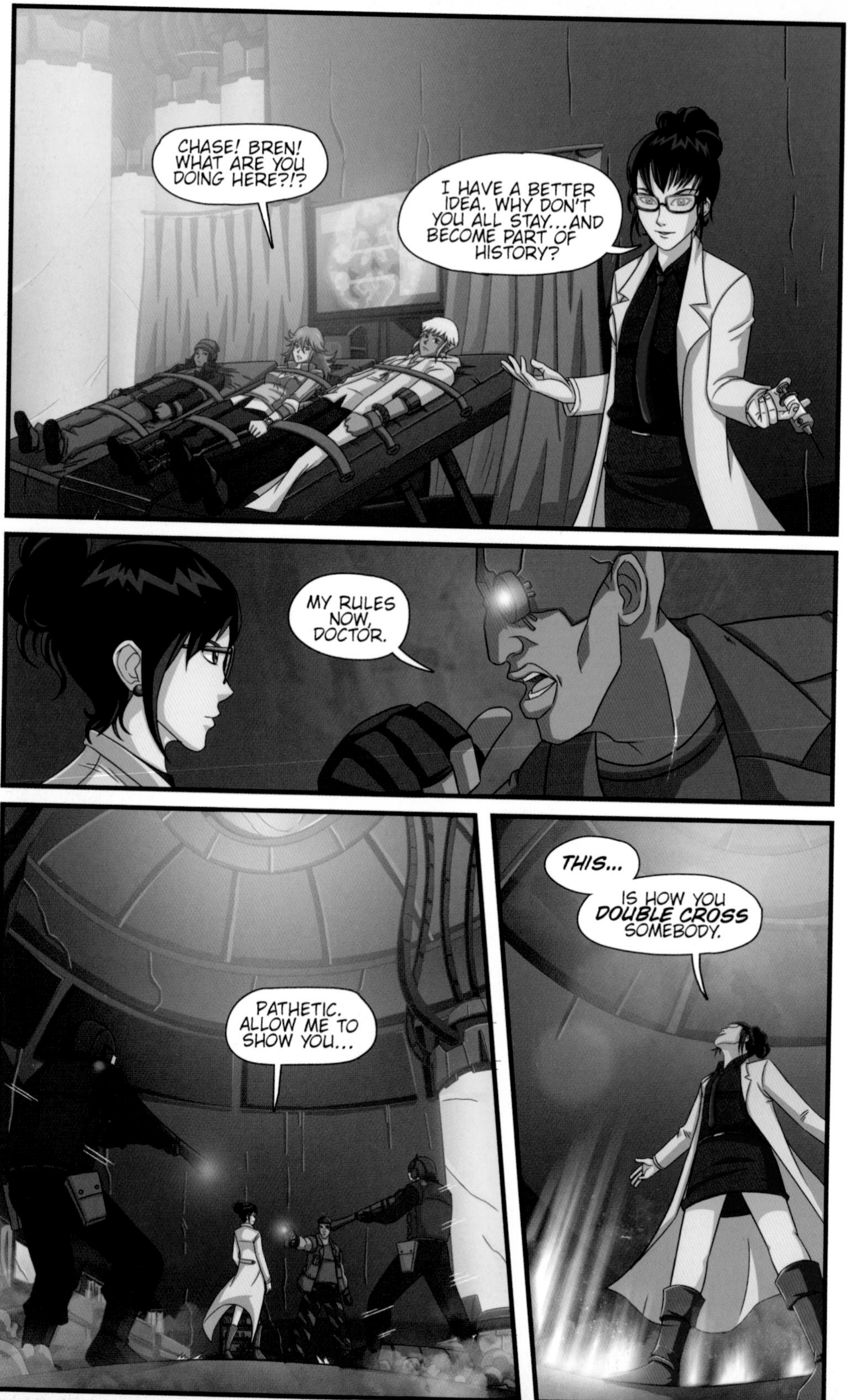
CHASE! BREN! WHAT ARE YOU DOING HERE?!?
I HAVE A BETTER IDEA. WHY DON'T YOU ALL STAY...AND BECOME PART OF HISTORY?
MY RULES NOW, DOCTOR.
PATHETIC. ALLOW ME TO SHOW YOU...
THIS...
IS HOW YOU DOUBLE CROSS SOMEBODY.

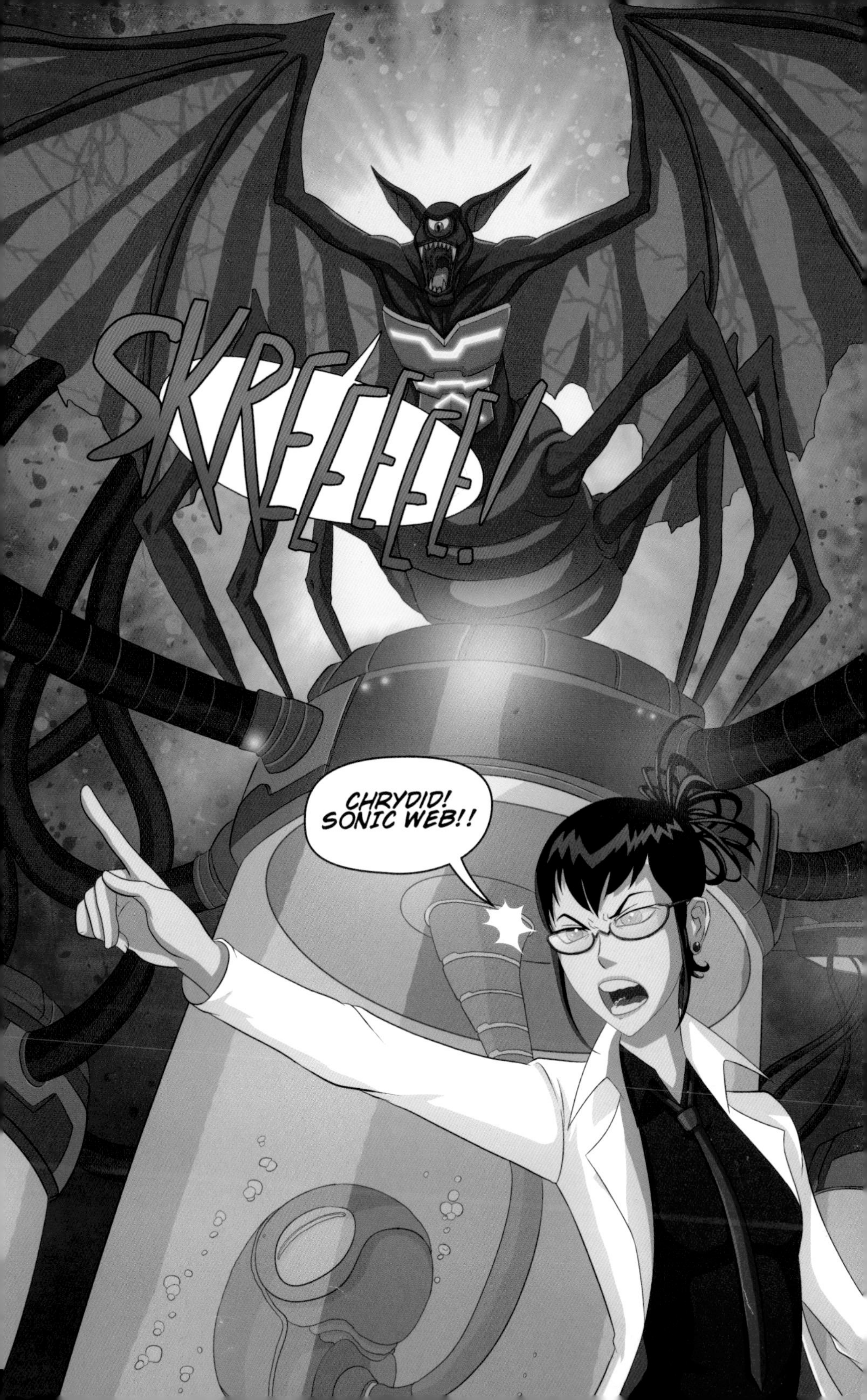
SKREEEEE!!
CHRYDID!
SONIC WEB!!

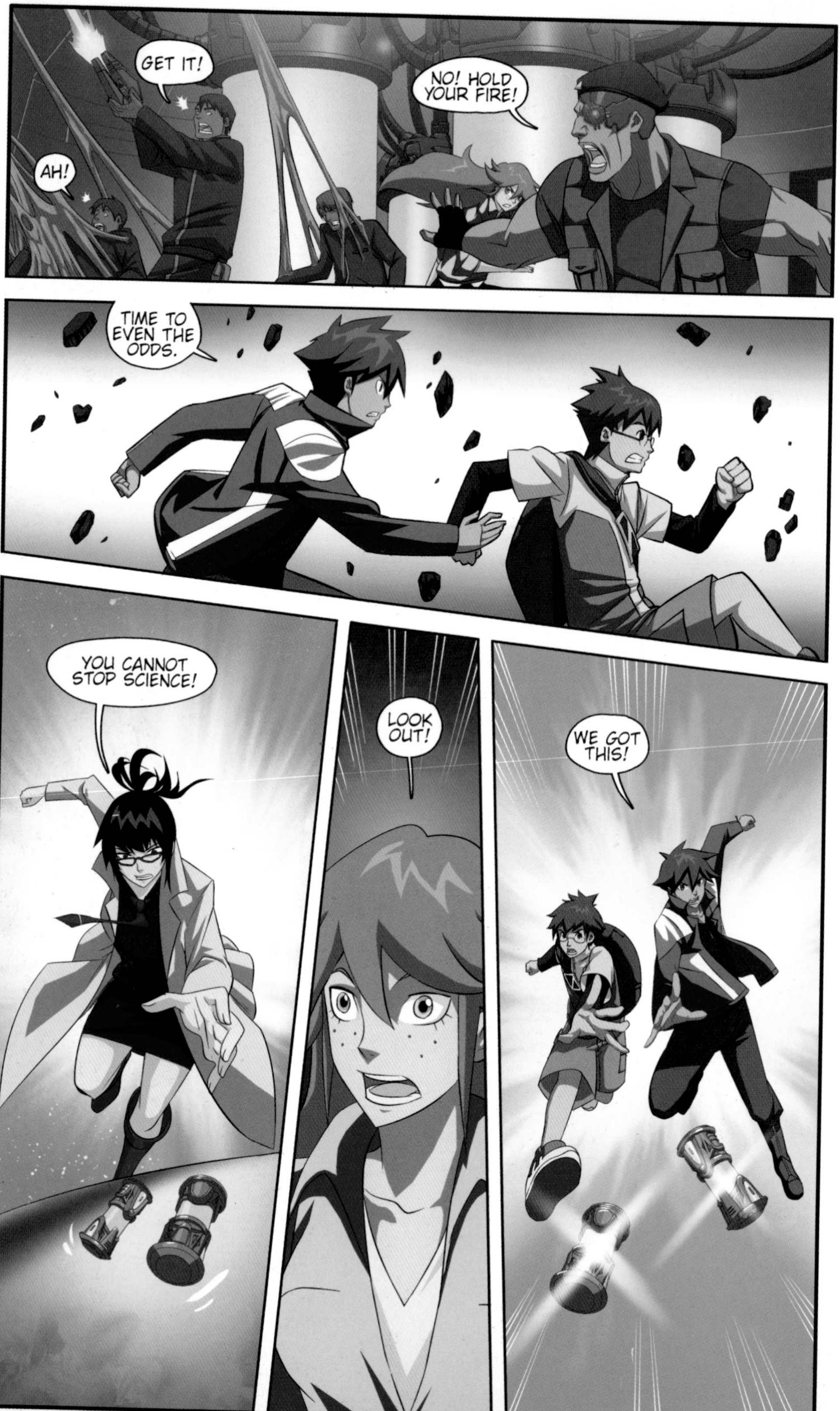
GET IT!
AH!
NO! HOLD YOUR FIRE!
TIME TO EVEN THE ODDS.
YOU CANNOT STOP SCIENCE!
LOOK OUT!
WE GOT THIS!

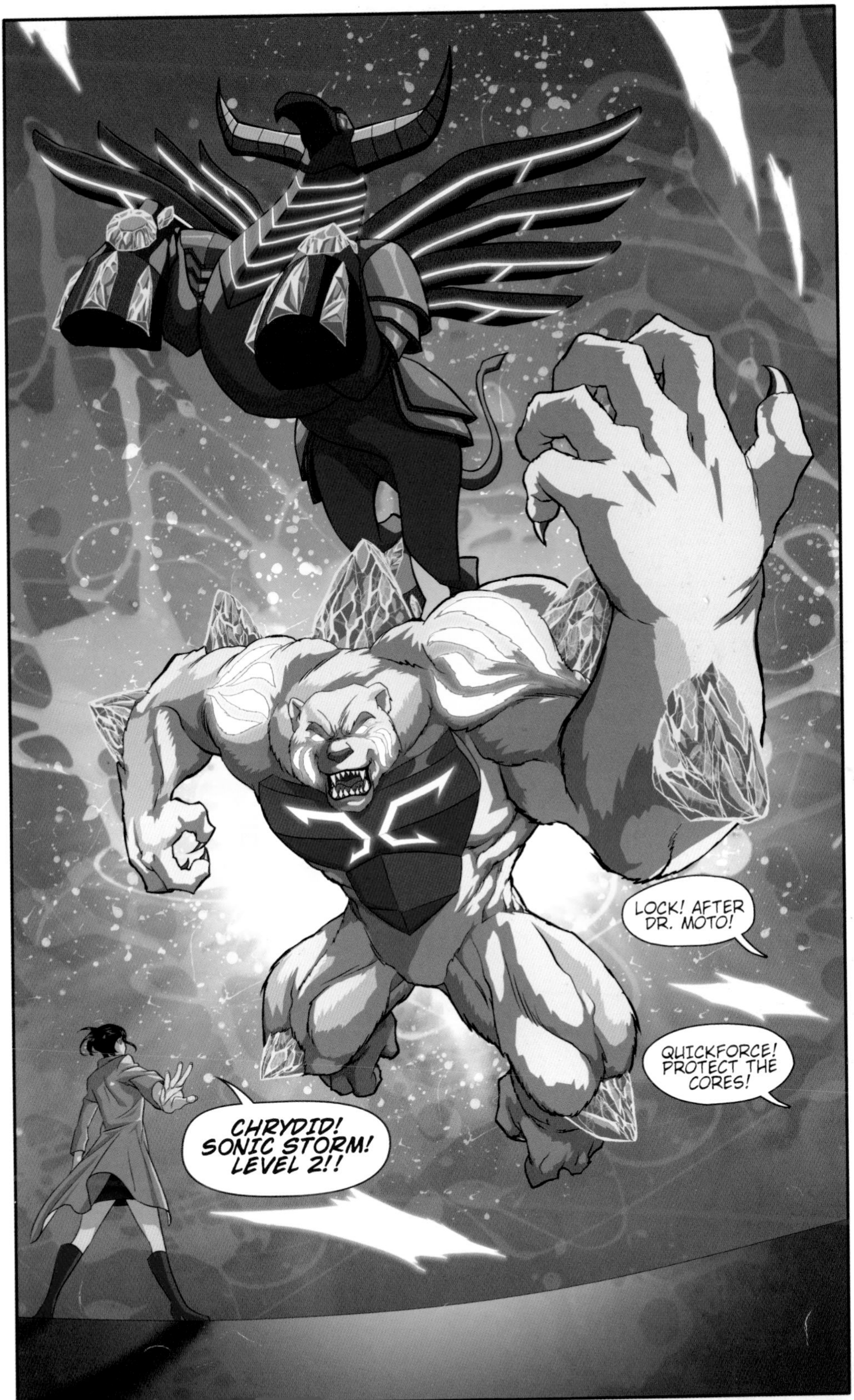
LOCK! AFTER DR. MOTO!
QUICKFORCE! PROTECT THE CORES!
CHRYDID! SONIC STORM! LEVEL 2!!

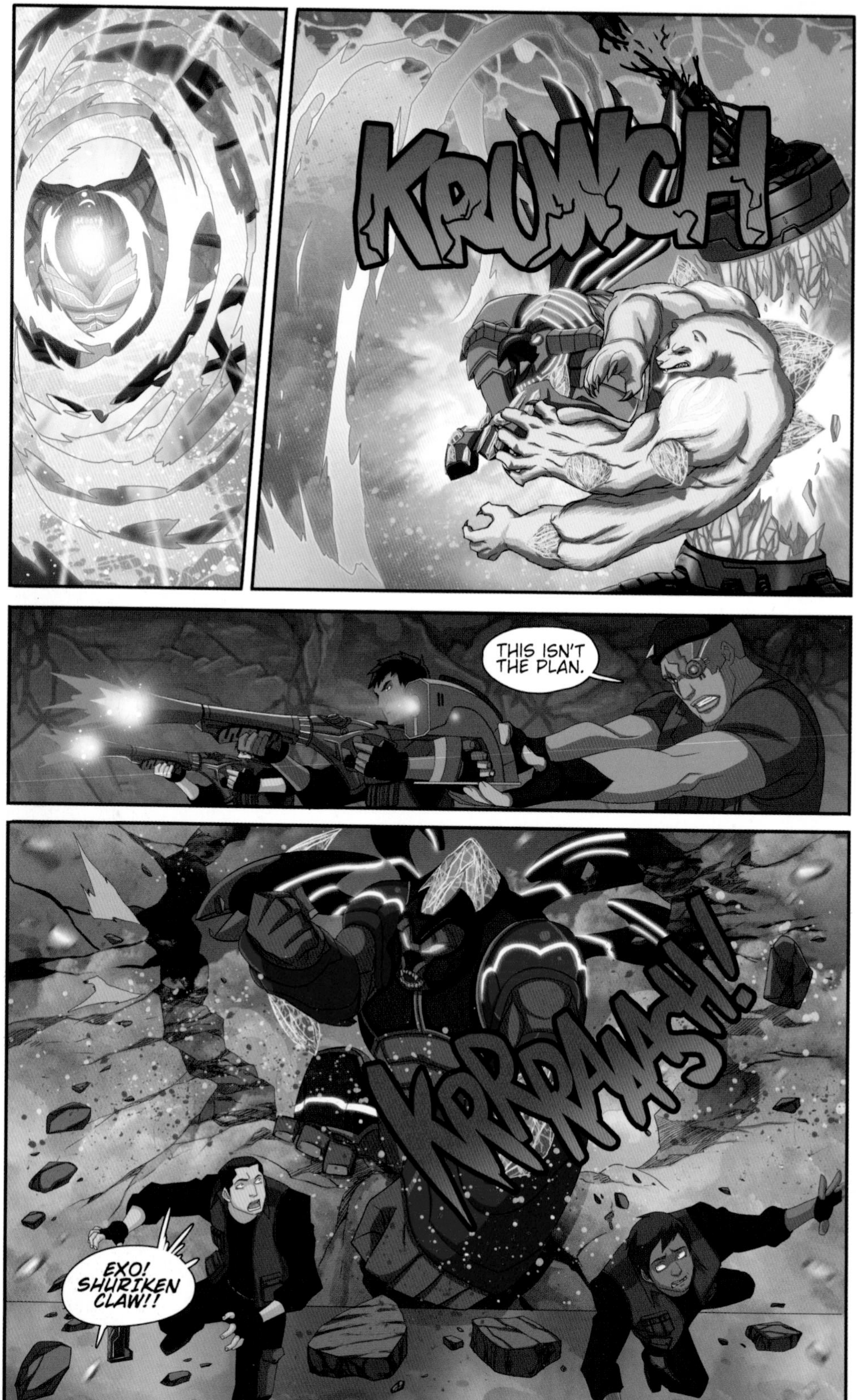
KRUNCH
THIS ISN'T THE PLAN.
KRRAASH!!
EXO! SHURIKEN CLAW!!

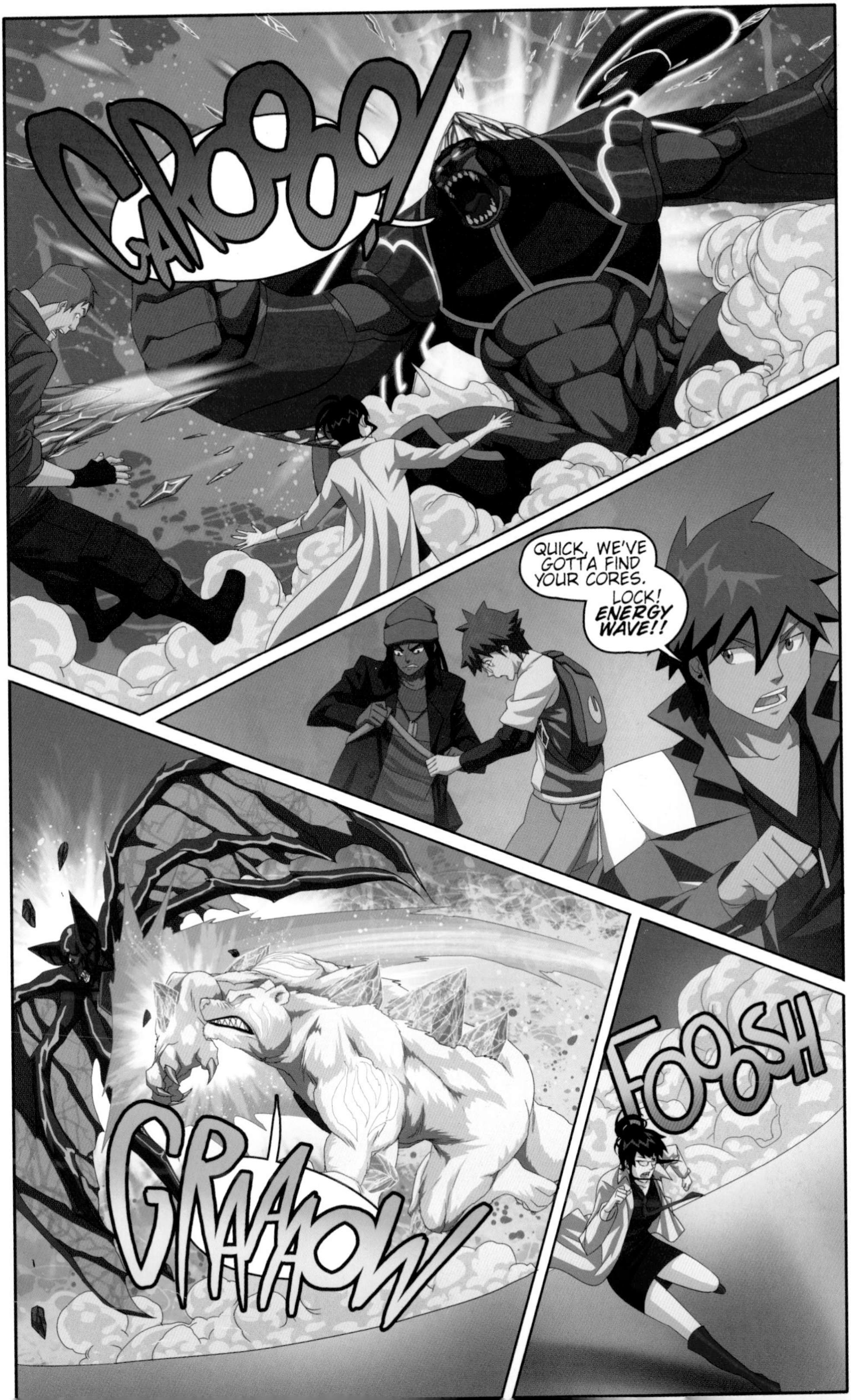
GAROOOOO
QUICK, WE'VE GOTTA FIND YOUR CORES.
LOCK! ENERGY WAVE!!
GRAAAOW
FOOOSH

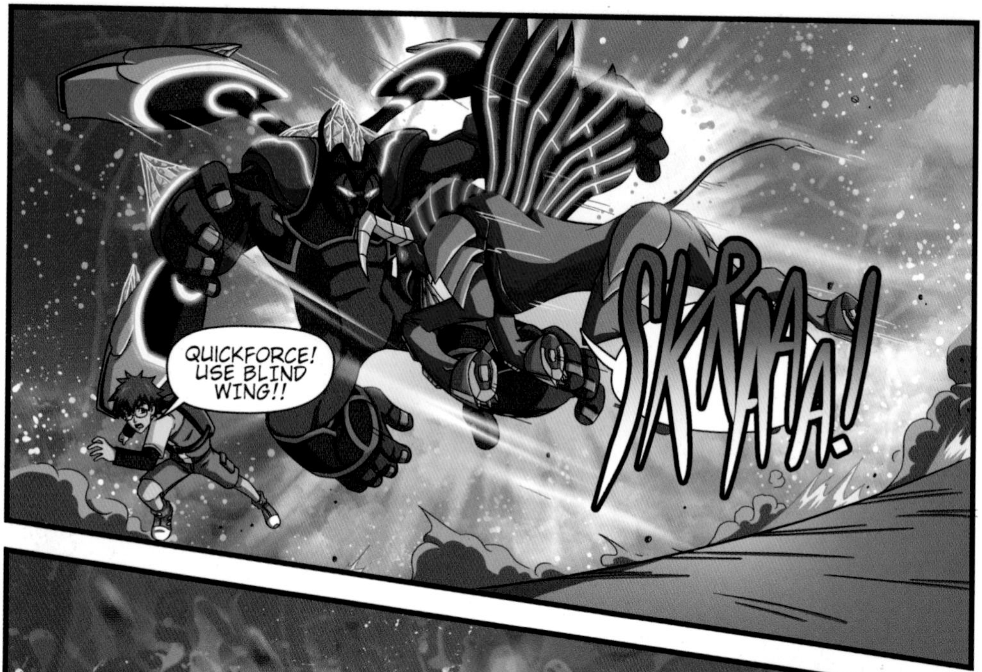
QUICKFORCE! USE BLIND WING!!
SKRAAA!
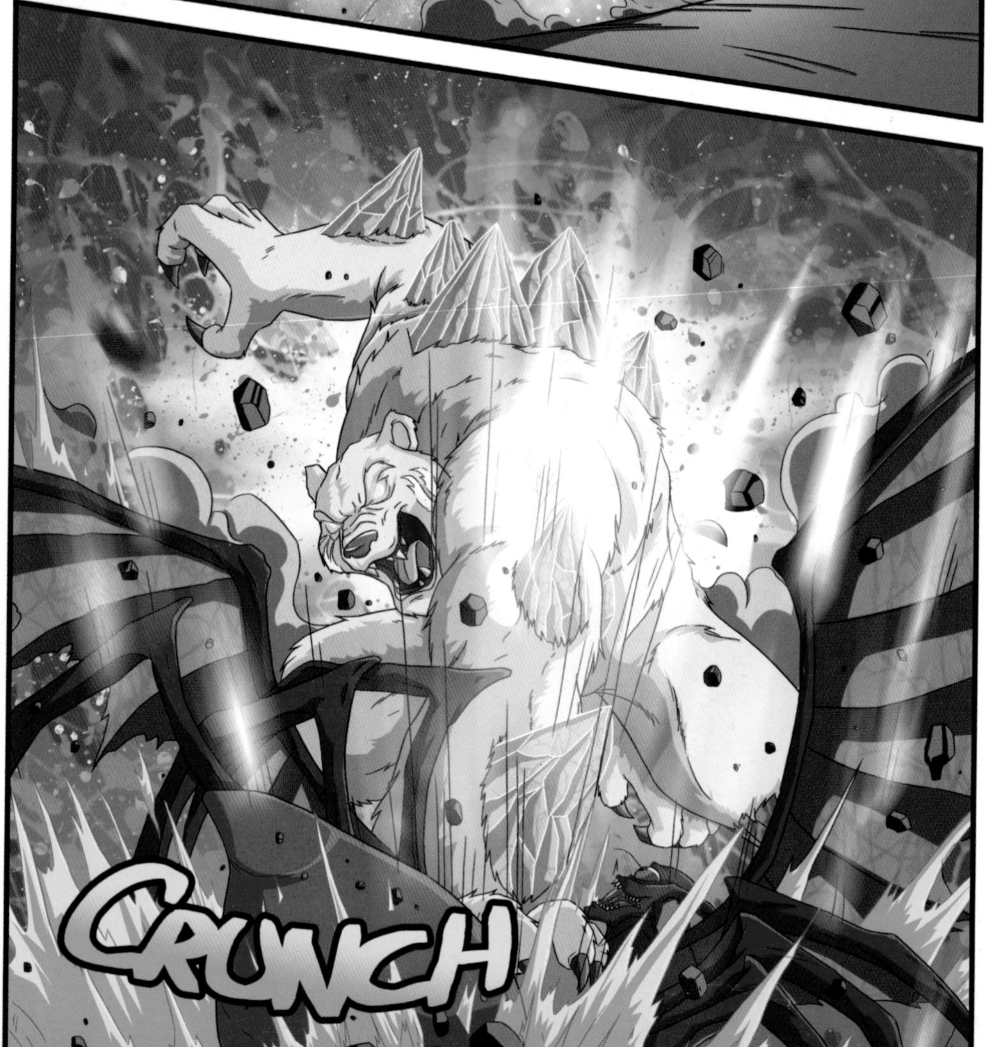
CRUNCH

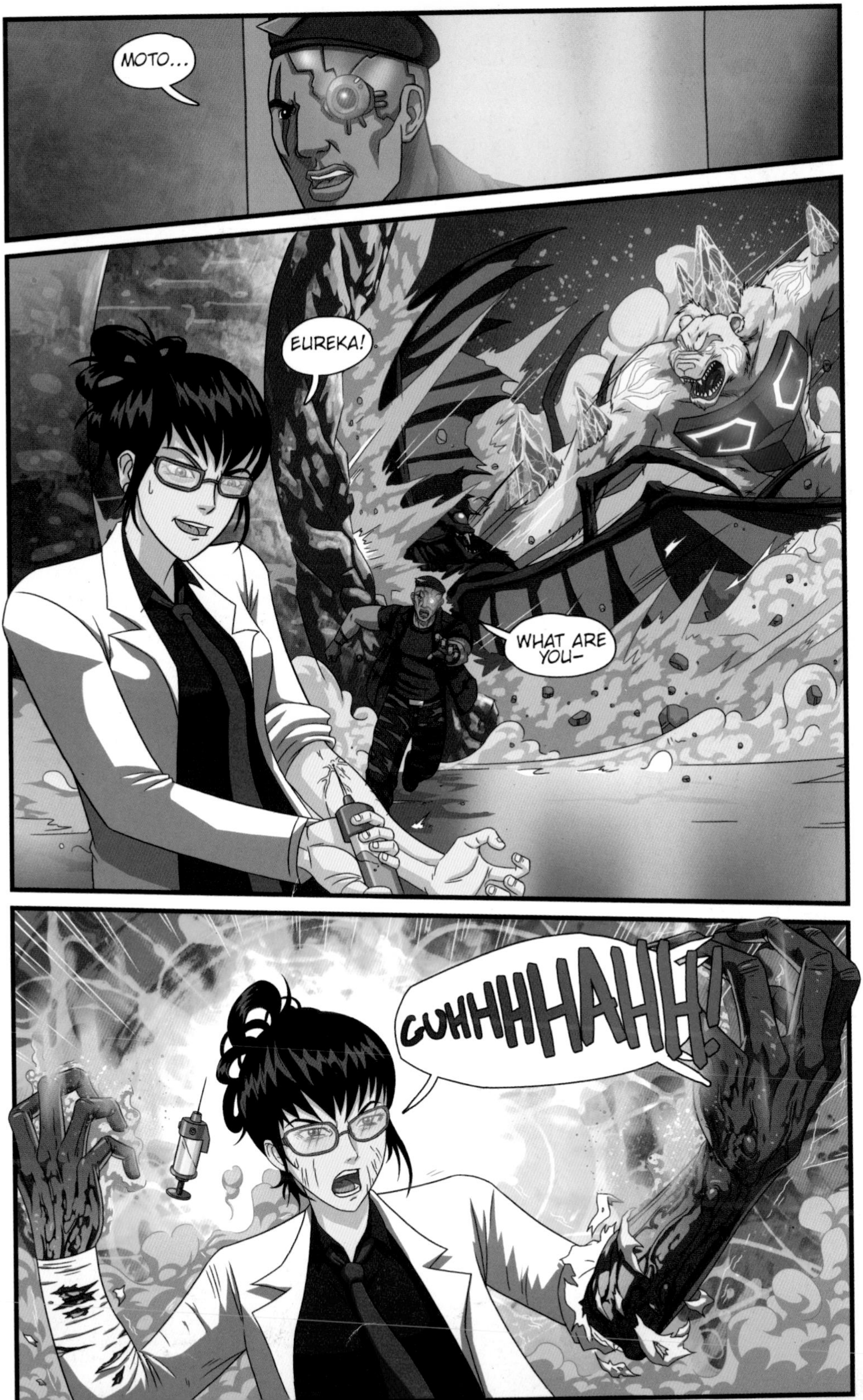
MOTO...
EUREKA!
WHAT ARE YOU-
GUHHHHAHH!

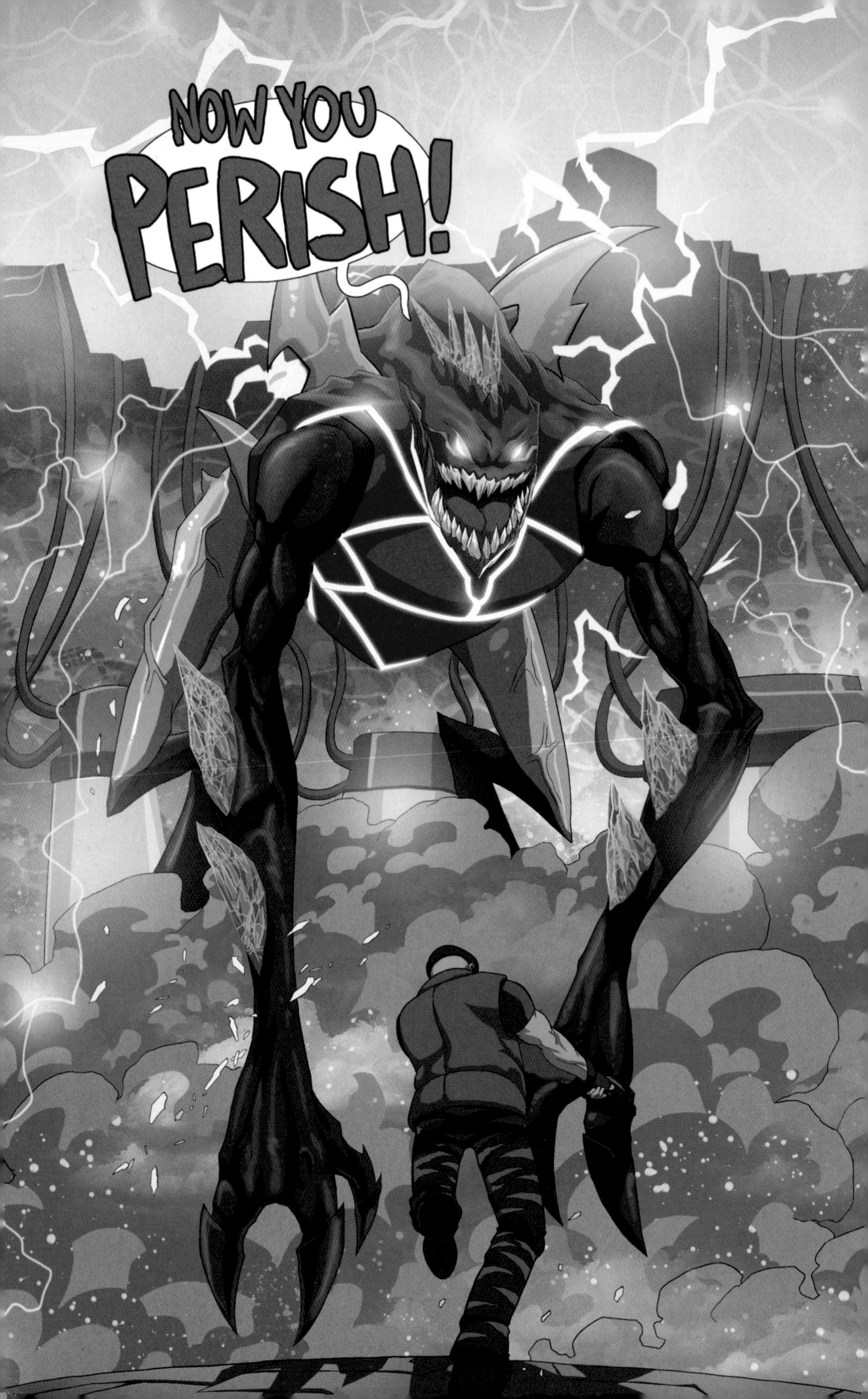
NOW YOU PERISH!

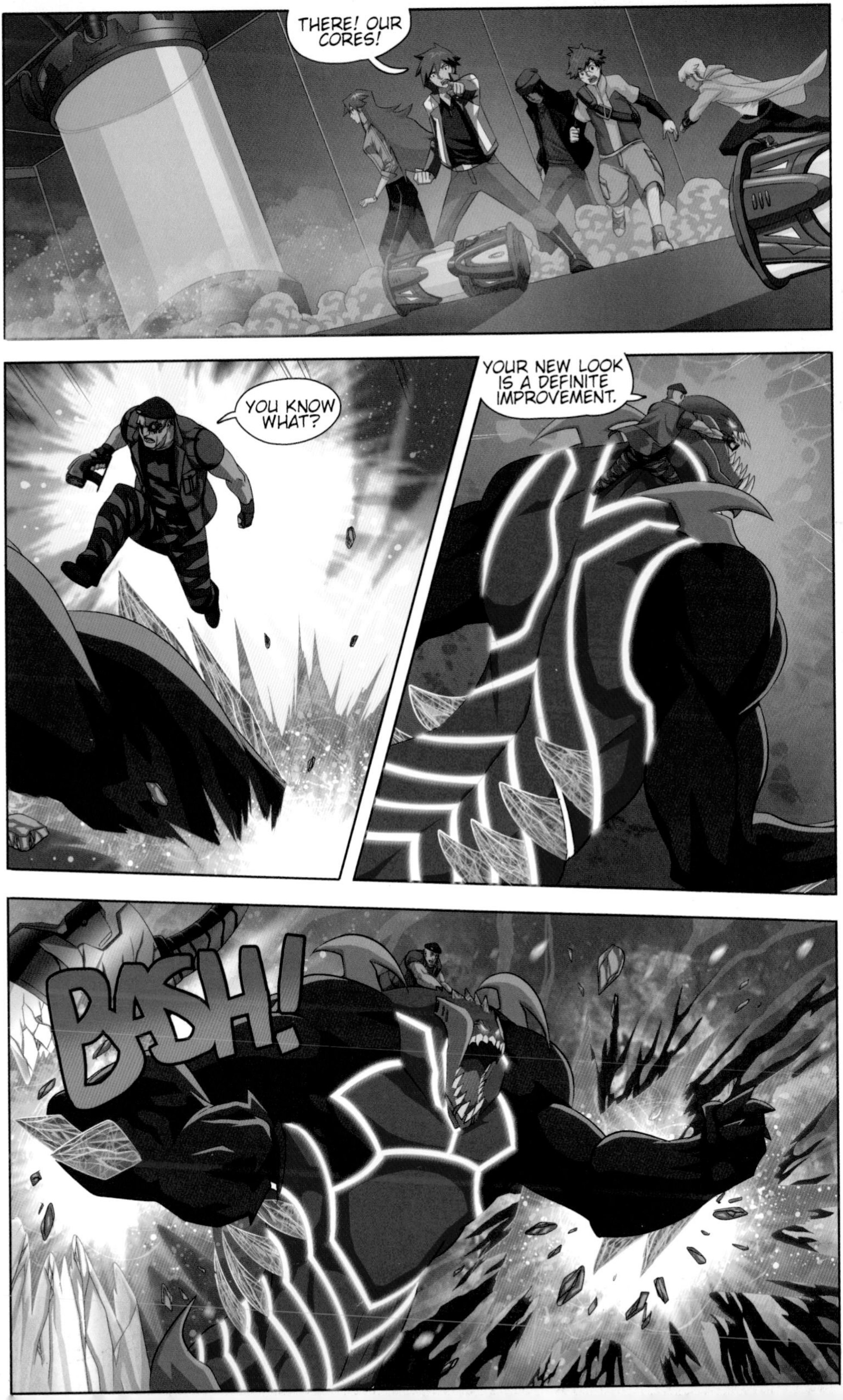
THERE! OUR CORES!
YOU KNOW WHAT?
YOUR NEW LOOK IS A DEFINITE IMPROVEMENT.
BASH!

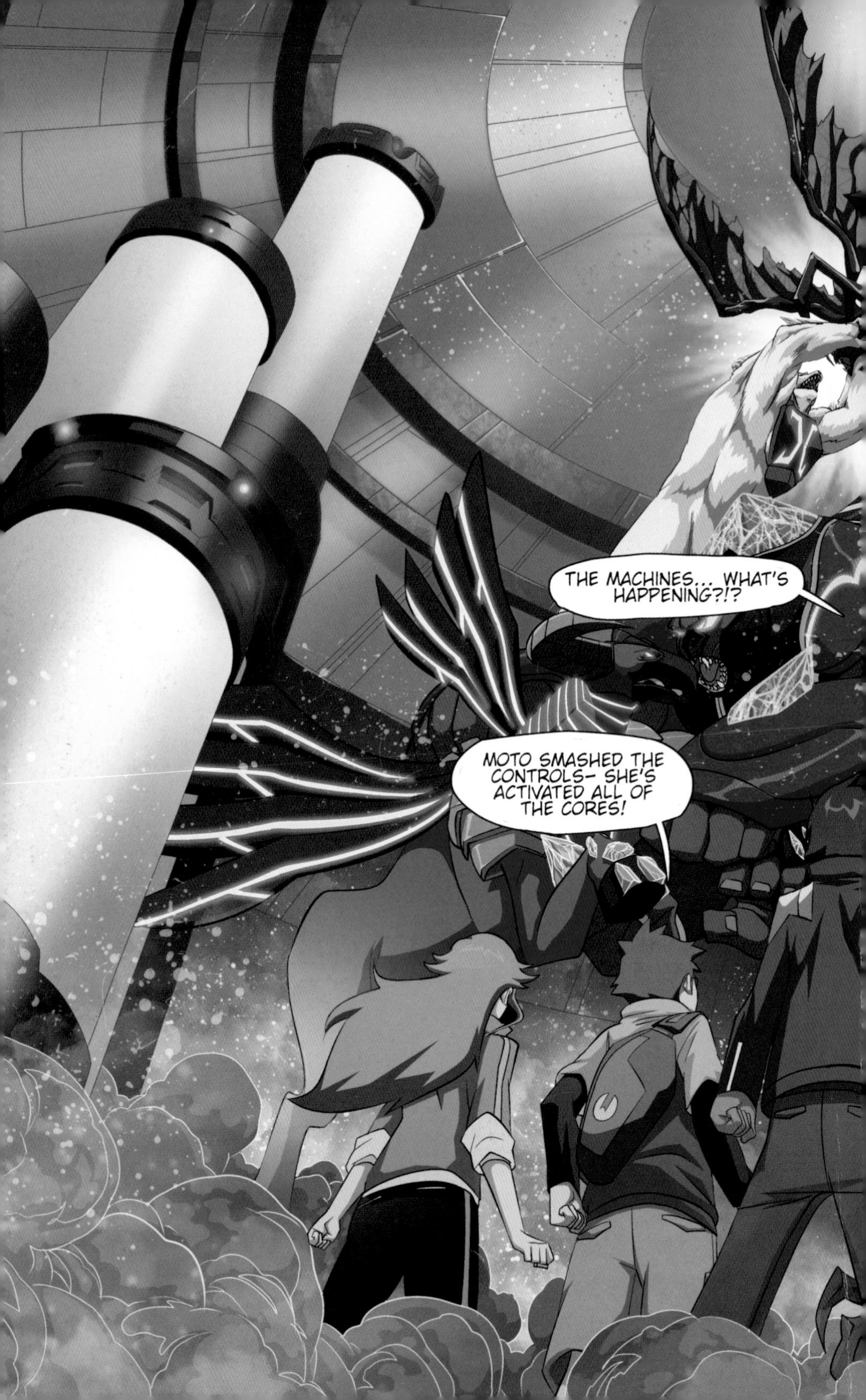
THE MACHINES... WHAT'S HAPPENING?!?
MOTO SMASHED THE CONTROLS- SHE'S ACTIVATED ALL OF THE CORES!

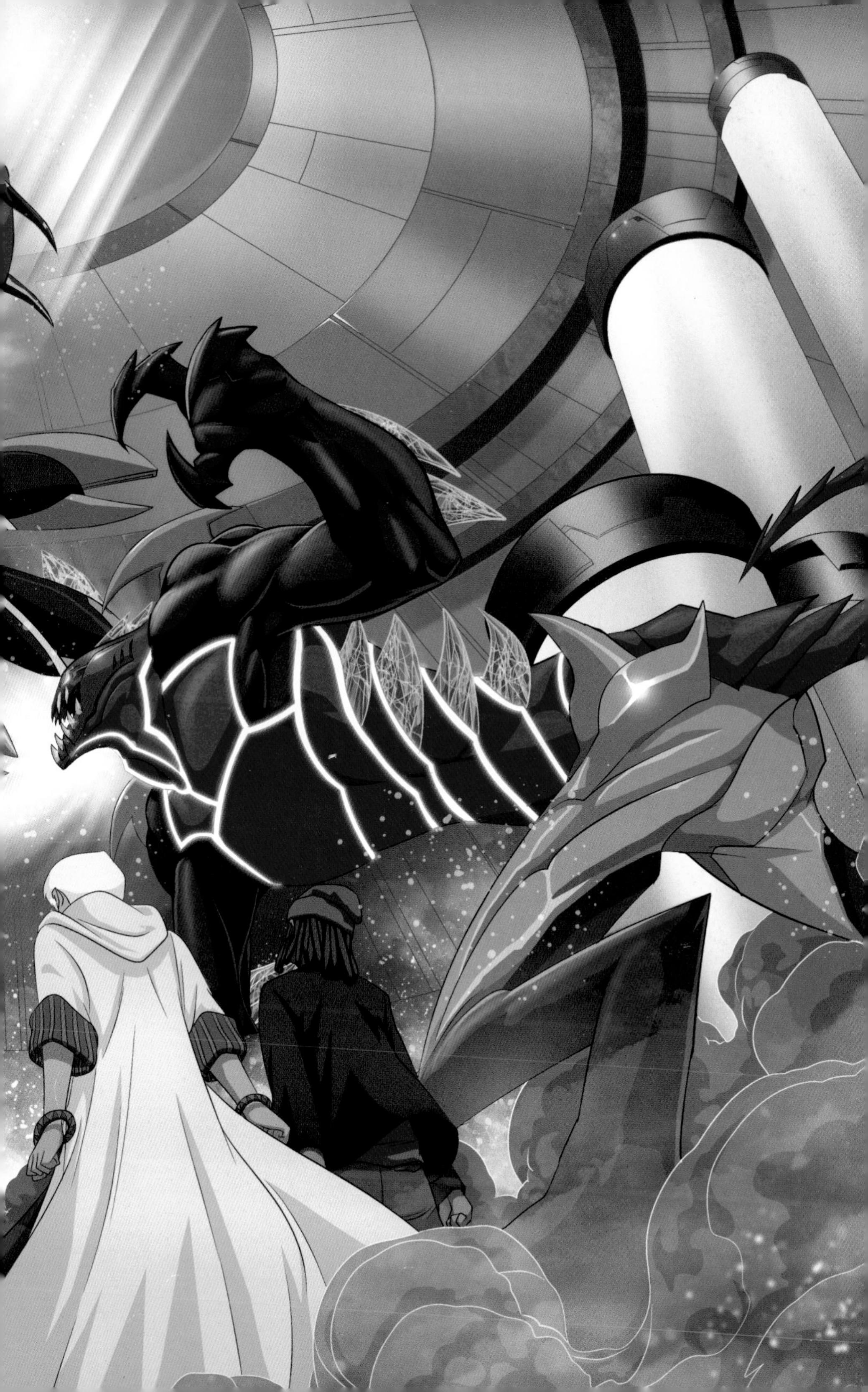

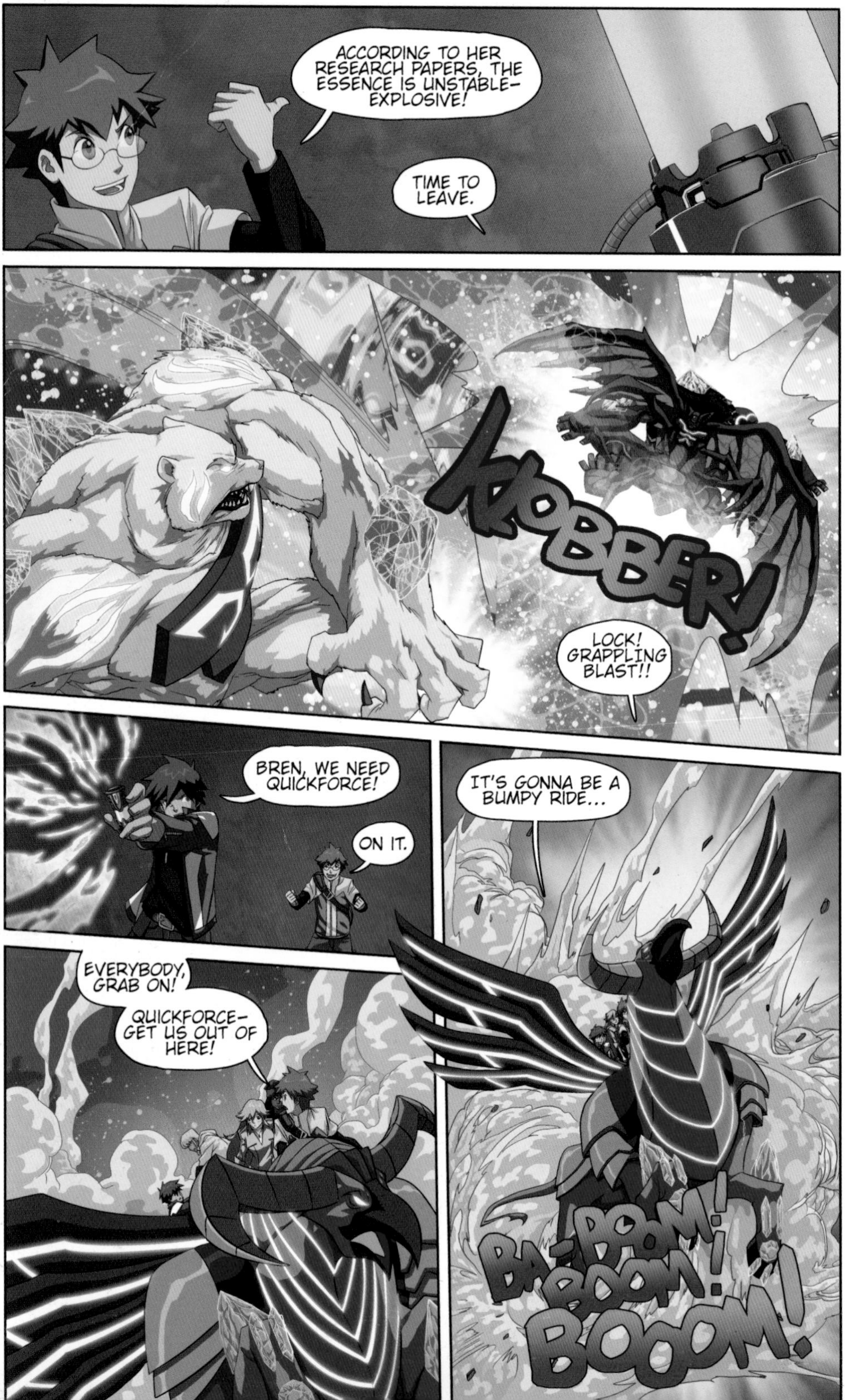
ACCORDING TO HER RESEARCH PAPERS, THE ESSENCE IS UNSTABLE-EXPLOSIVE!
TIME TO LEAVE.
KROBBER!
LOCK! GRAPPLING BLAST!!
BREN, WE NEED QUICKFORCE!
ON IT.
IT'S GONNA BE A BUMPY RIDE...
EVERYBODY, GRAB ON!
QUICKFORCE-GET US OUT OF HERE!
BA-BOOM! BOOM! BOOOM!

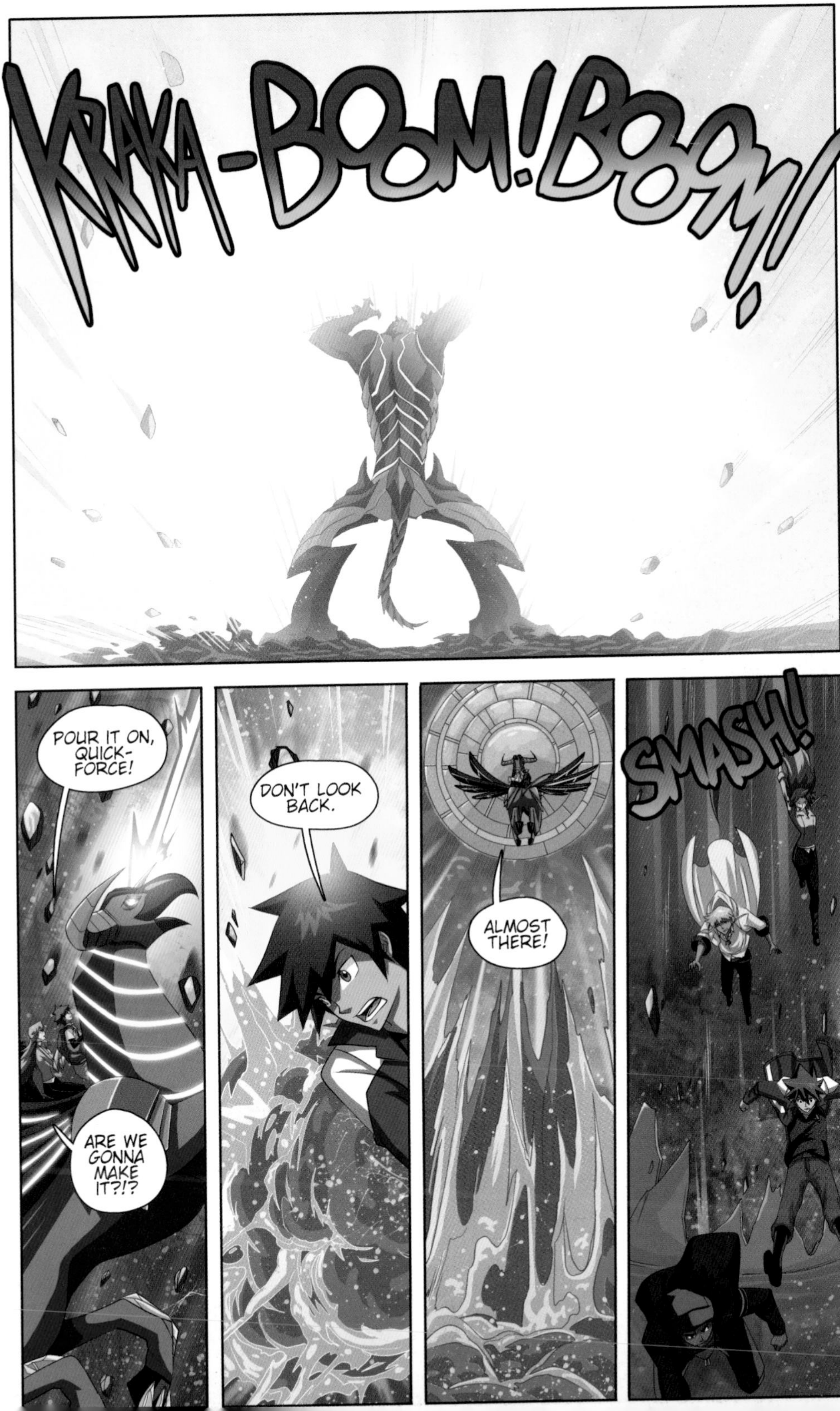
KRAKA-BOOM! BOOM!!
POUR IT ON, QUICK-FORCE!
ARE WE GONNA MAKE IT?!?
DON'T LOOK BACK.
ALMOST THERE!
SMASH!

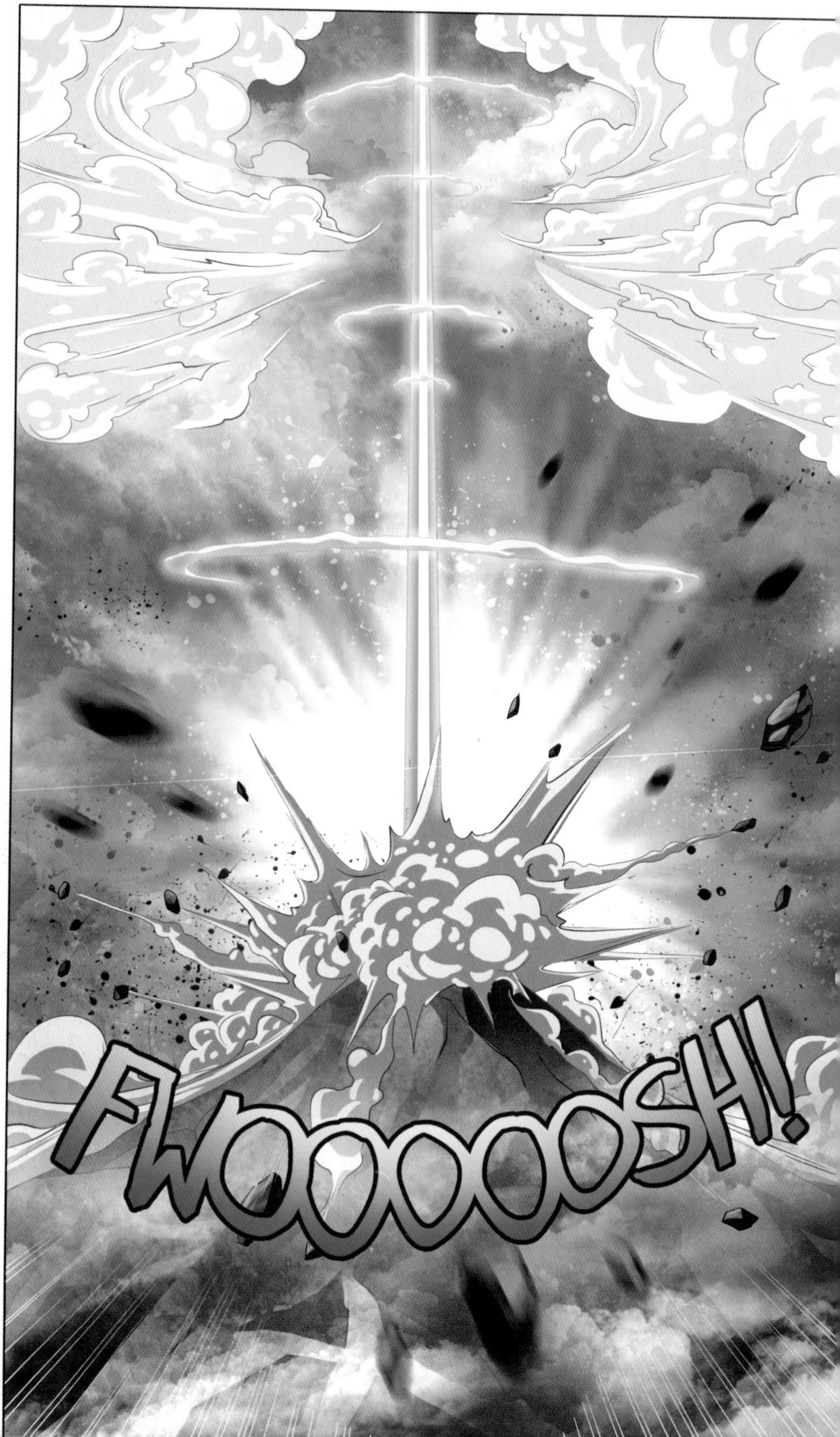
FWOOOOOSH!

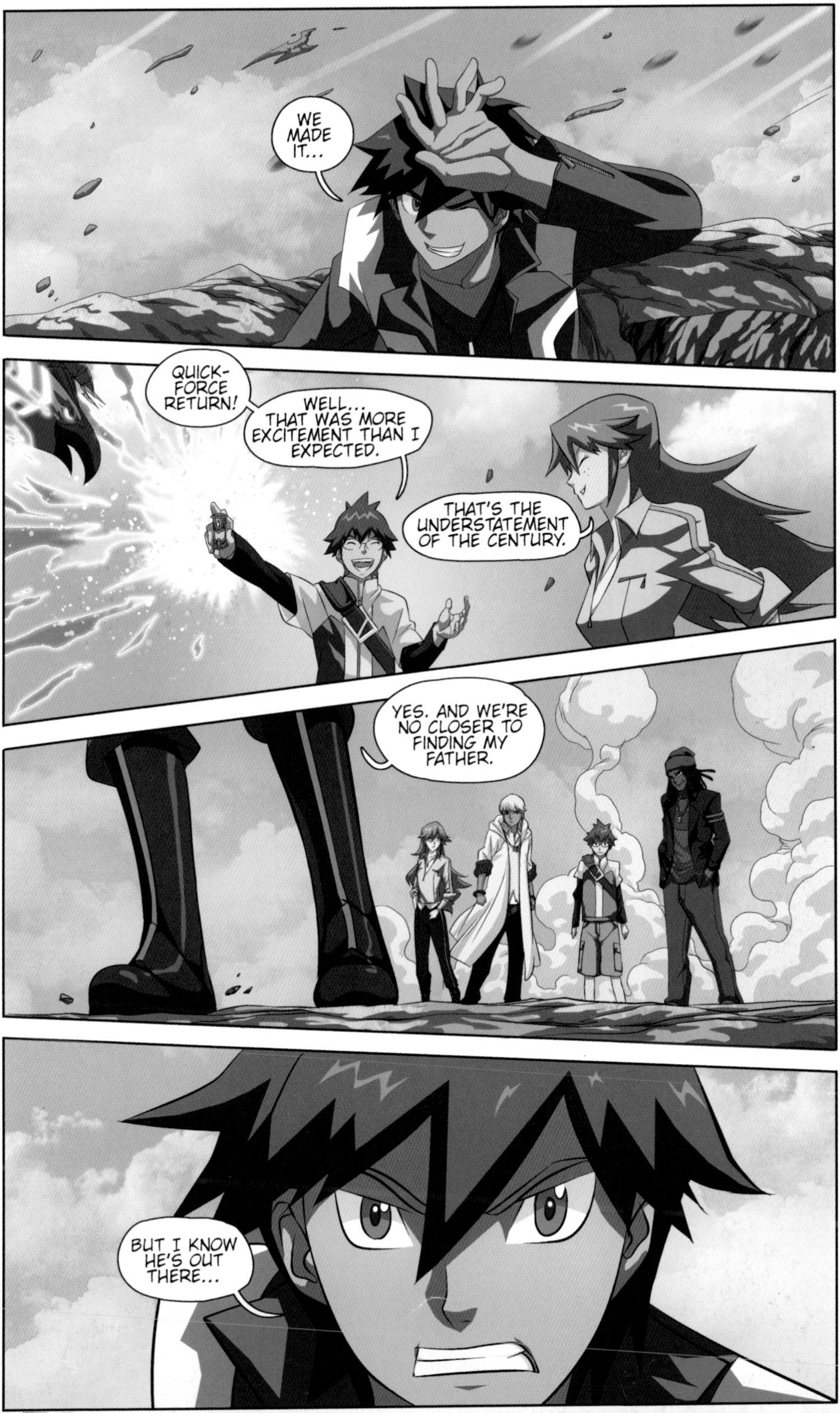
WE MADE IT...
QUICK-FORCE RETURN!
WELL... THAT WAS MORE EXCITEMENT THAN I EXPECTED.
THAT'S THE UNDERSTATEMENT OF THE CENTURY.
YES. AND WE'RE NO CLOSER TO FINDING MY FATHER.
BUT I KNOW HE'S OUT THERE...

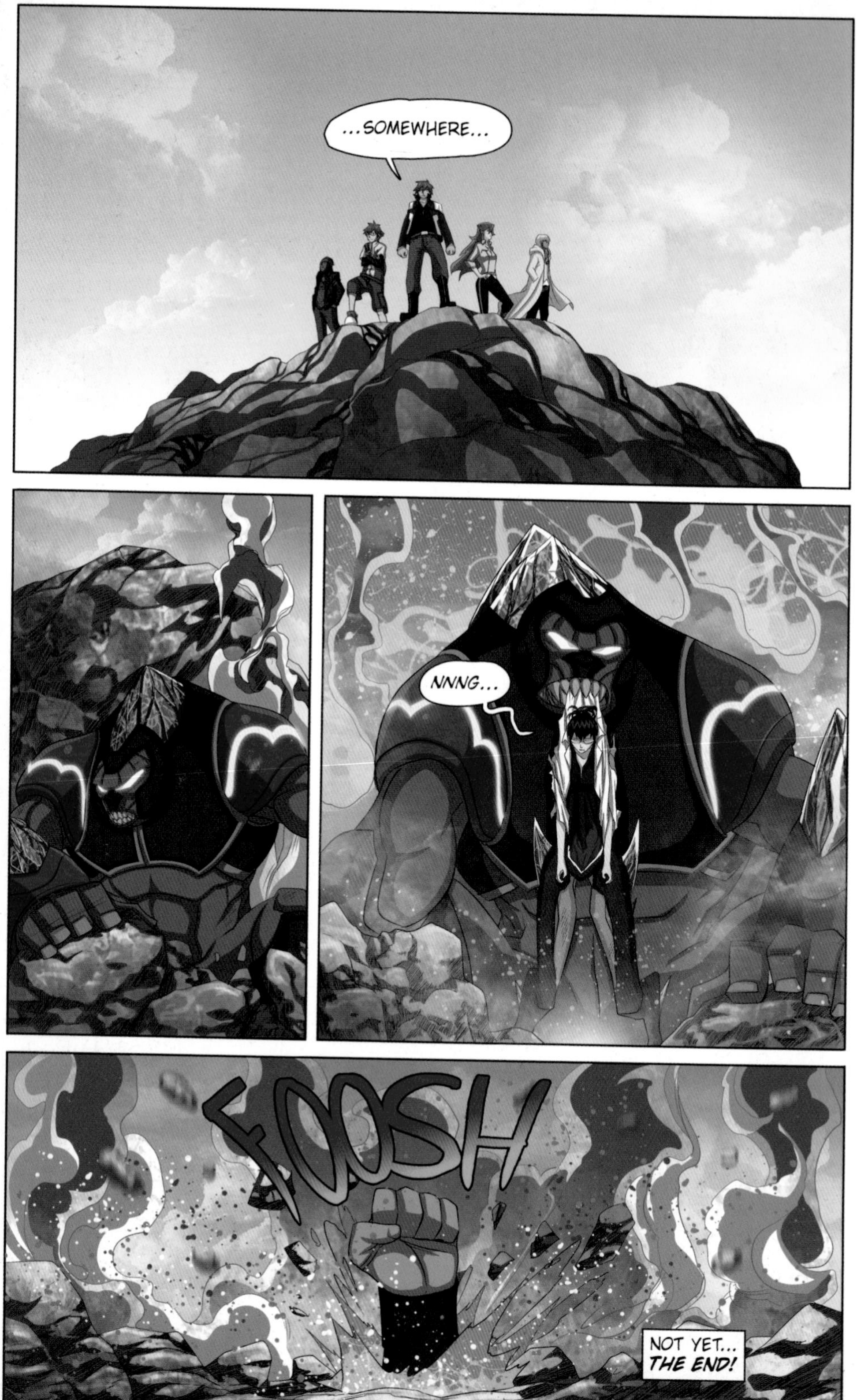
...SOMEWHERE...
NNNG...
FOOSH
NOT YET...
THE END!

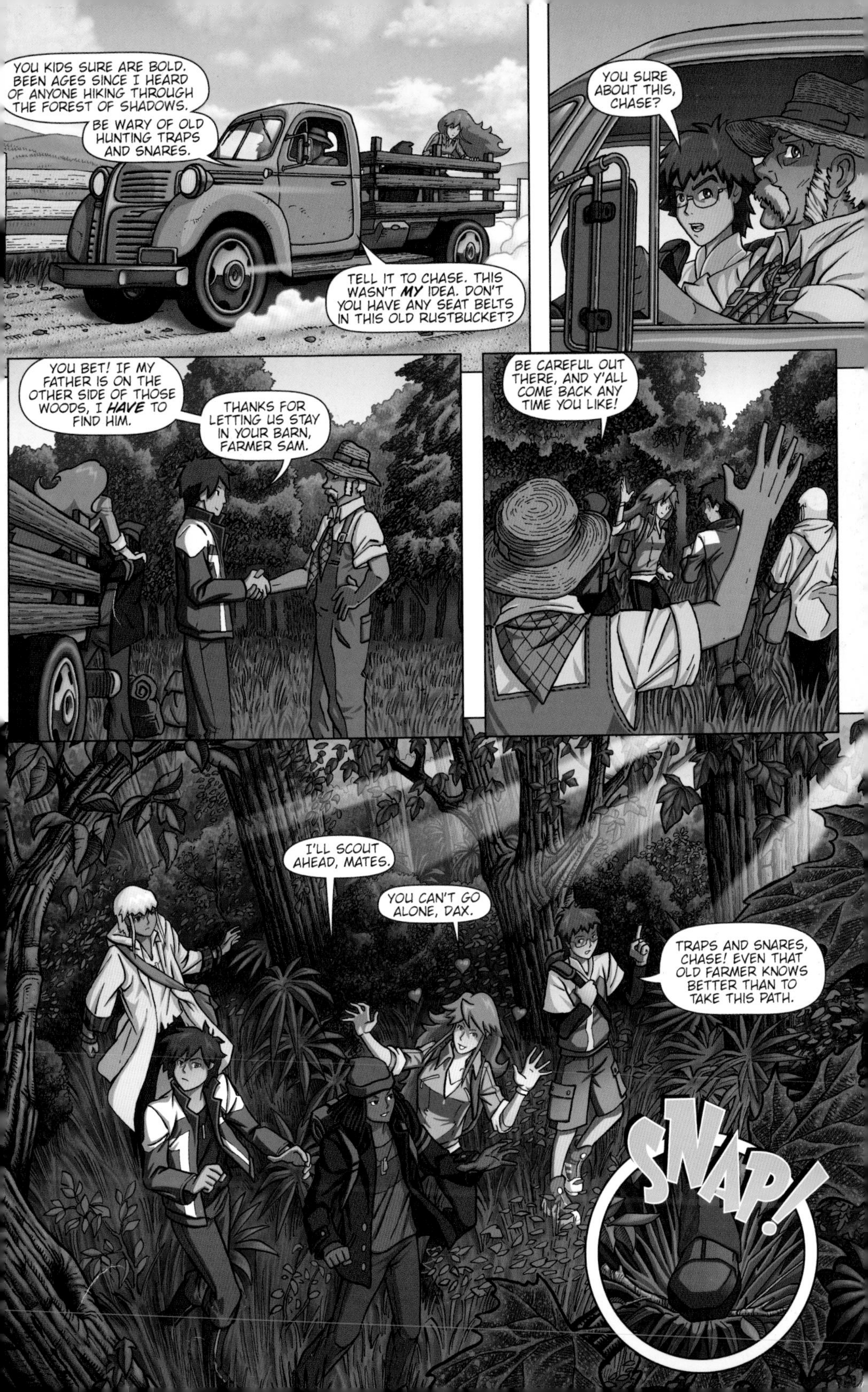
YOU KIDS SURE ARE BOLD. BEEN AGES SINCE I HEARD OF ANYONE HIKING THROUGH THE FOREST OF SHADOWS.
BE WARY OF OLD HUNTING TRAPS AND SNARES.
TELL IT TO CHASE. THIS WASN'T MY IDEA. DON'T YOU HAVE ANY SEAT BELTS IN THIS OLD RUSTBUCKET?
YOU SURE ABOUT THIS, CHASE?
YOU BET! IF MY FATHER IS ON THE OTHER SIDE OF THOSE WOODS, I HAVE TO FIND HIM.
THANKS FOR LETTING US STAY IN YOUR BARN, FARMER SAM.
BE CAREFUL OUT THERE, AND Y'ALL COME BACK ANY TIME YOU LIKE!
I'LL SCOUT AHEAD, MATES.
YOU CAN'T GO ALONE, DAX.
TRAPS AND SNARES, CHASE! EVEN THAT OLD FARMER KNOWS BETTER THAN TO TAKE THIS PATH.
SNAP!

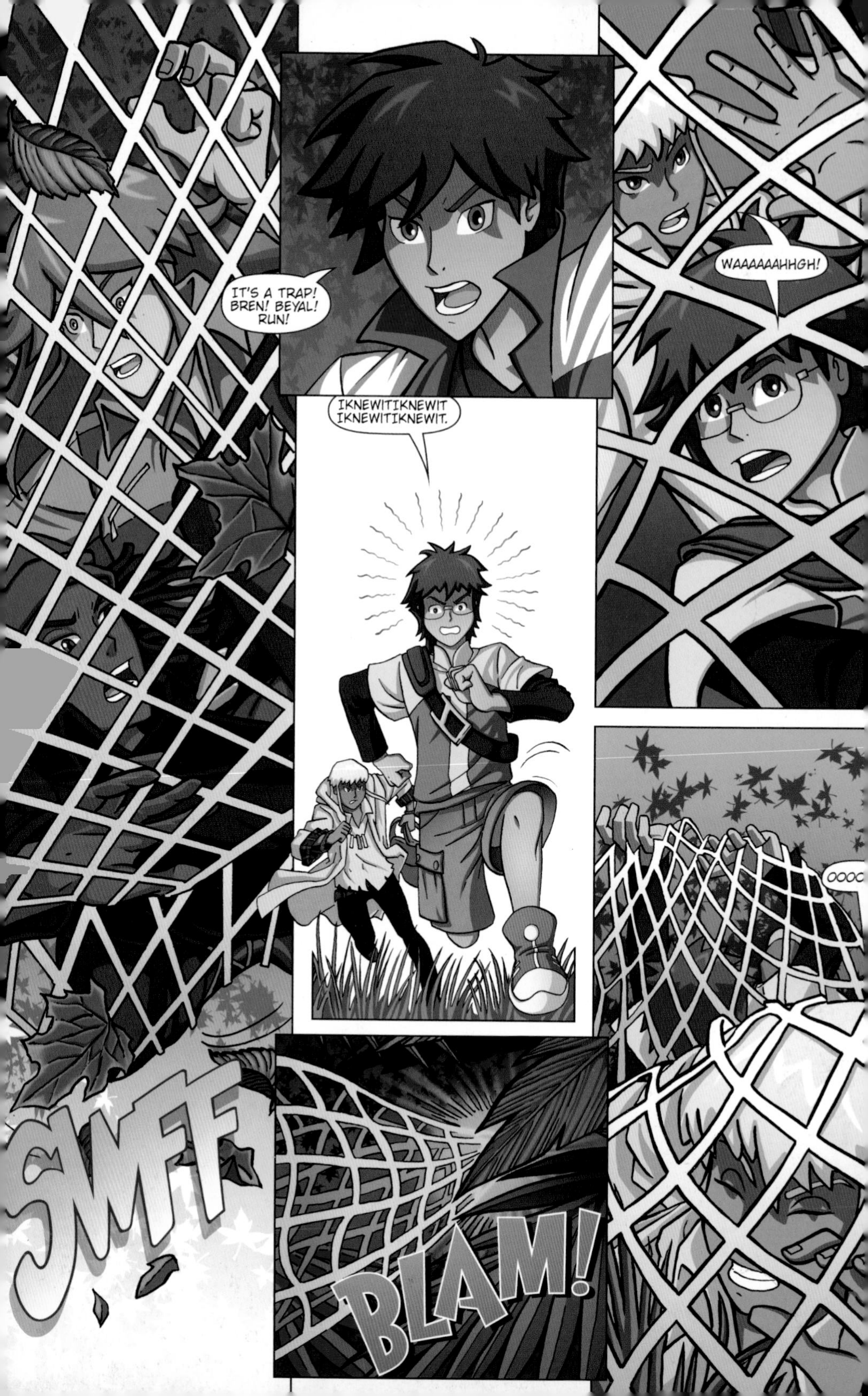
IT'S A TRAP! BREN! BEYAL! RUN!
WAAAAAAHHGH!
IKNEWITIKNEWIT IKNEWITIKNEWIT.
OOOO
SMFF
BLAM!

SACRIFICE

Story by **Cory Levine**
Art by **Maurizio Campidelli**
Letters & Additional Colors by **Zack Turner**

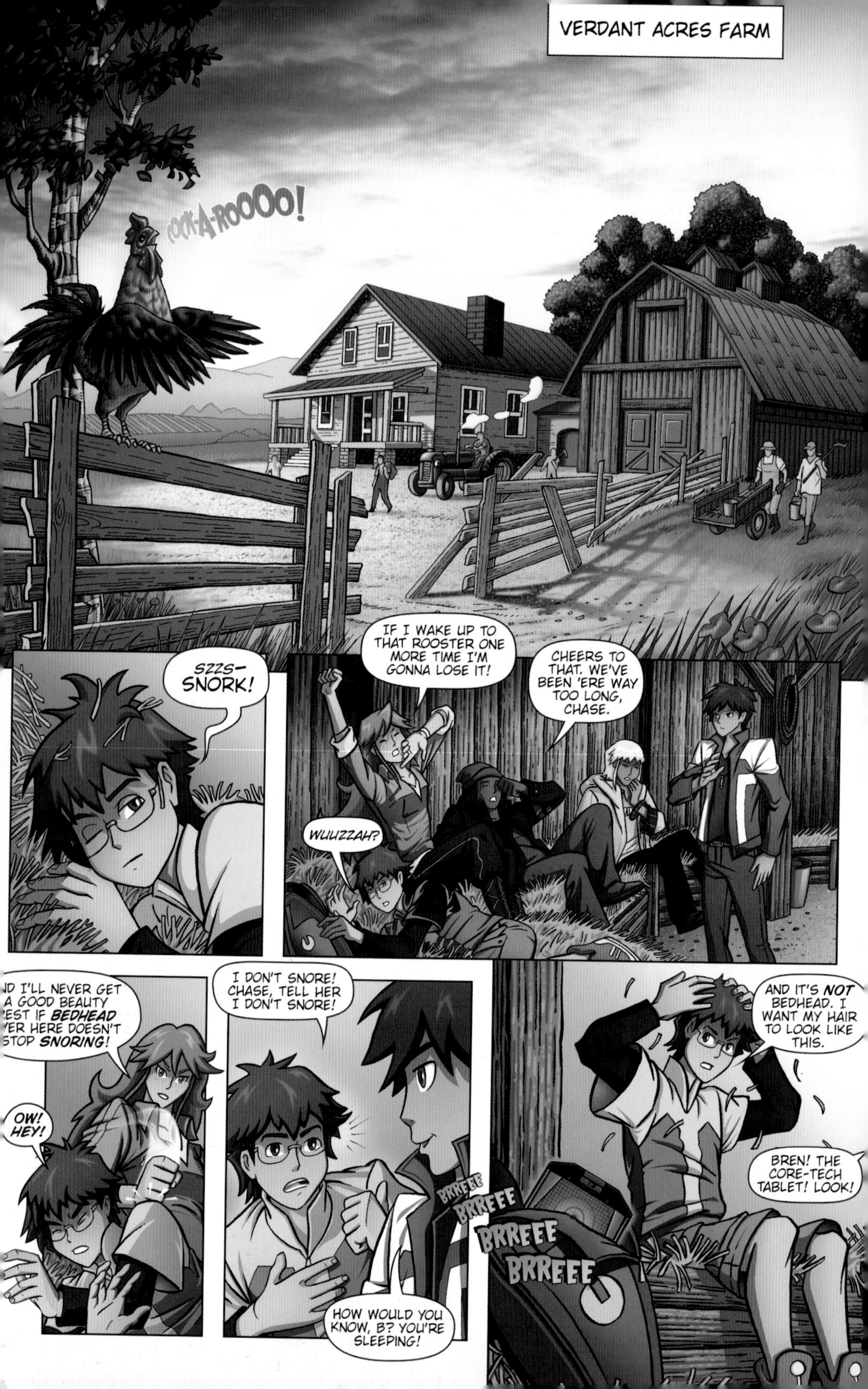
VERDANT ACRES FARM
COCK-A-ROOOO!
SZZS-SNORK!
IF I WAKE UP TO THAT ROOSTER ONE MORE TIME I'M GONNA LOSE IT!
CHEERS TO THAT. WE'VE BEEN 'ERE WAY TOO LONG, CHASE.
WUUZZAH?
ND I'LL NEVER GET A GOOD BEAUTY REST IF BEDHEAD VER HERE DOESN'T STOP SNORING!
OW! HEY!
I DON'T SNORE! CHASE, TELL HER I DON'T SNORE!
HOW WOULD YOU KNOW, B? YOU'RE SLEEPING!
BRREEE BRREEE BRREEE BRREEE
AND IT'S NOT BEDHEAD. I WANT MY HAIR TO LOOK LIKE THIS.
BREN! THE CORE-TECH TABLET! LOOK!

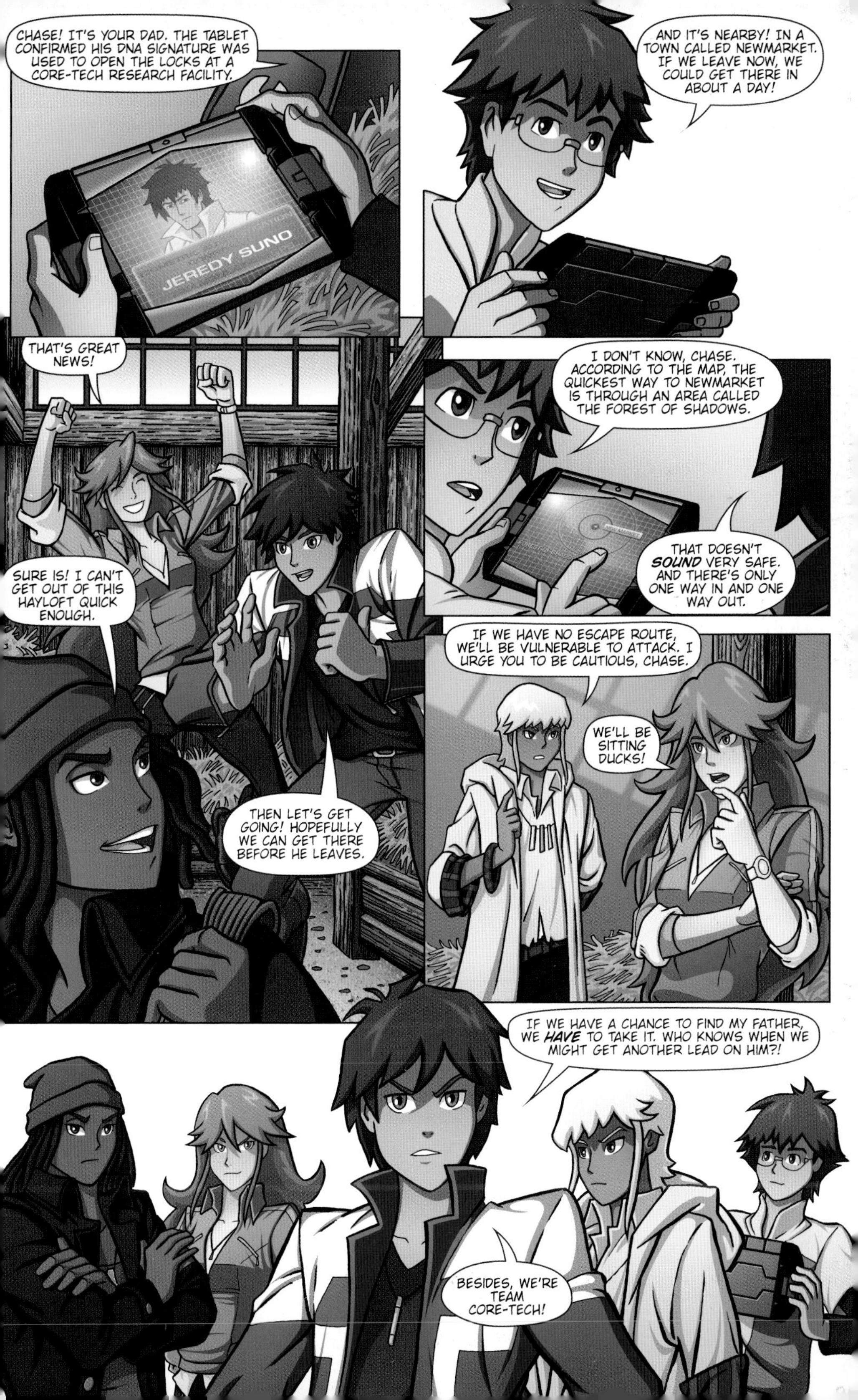
CHASE! IT'S YOUR DAD. THE TABLET CONFIRMED HIS DNA SIGNATURE WAS USED TO OPEN THE LOCKS AT A CORE-TECH RESEARCH FACILITY.
JEREDY SUNO
AND IT'S NEARBY! IN A TOWN CALLED NEWMARKET. IF WE LEAVE NOW, WE COULD GET THERE IN ABOUT A DAY!
THAT'S GREAT NEWS!
SURE IS! I CAN'T GET OUT OF THIS HAYLOFT QUICK ENOUGH.
THEN LET'S GET GOING! HOPEFULLY WE CAN GET THERE BEFORE HE LEAVES.
I DON'T KNOW, CHASE. ACCORDING TO THE MAP, THE QUICKEST WAY TO NEWMARKET IS THROUGH AN AREA CALLED THE FOREST OF SHADOWS.
THAT DOESN'T SOUND VERY SAFE. AND THERE'S ONLY ONE WAY IN AND ONE WAY OUT.
IF WE HAVE NO ESCAPE ROUTE, WE'LL BE VULNERABLE TO ATTACK. I URGE YOU TO BE CAUTIOUS, CHASE.
WE'LL BE SITTING DUCKS!
IF WE HAVE A CHANCE TO FIND MY FATHER, WE HAVE TO TAKE IT. WHO KNOWS WHEN WE MIGHT GET ANOTHER LEAD ON HIM?!
BESIDES, WE'RE TEAM CORE-TECH!

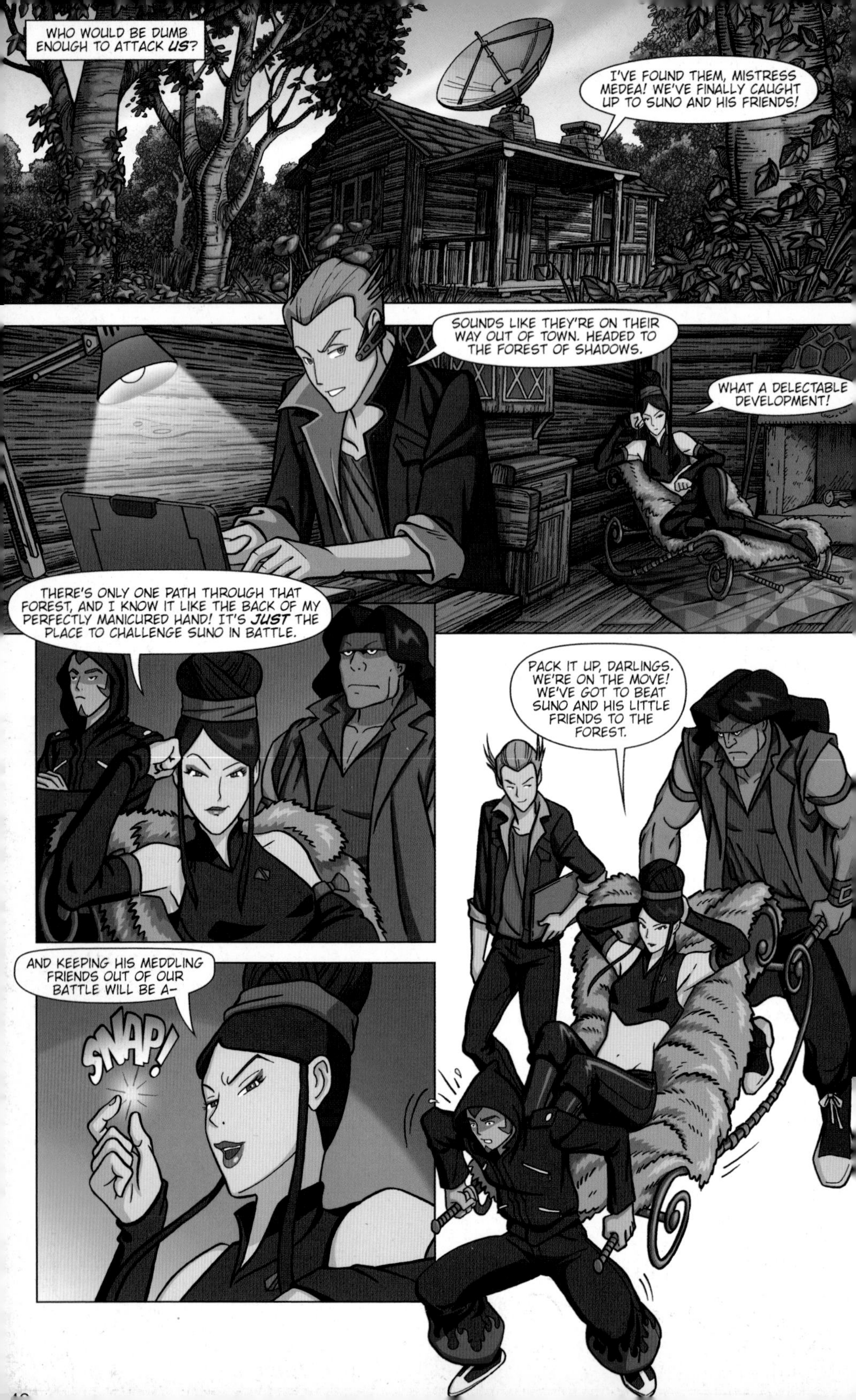
WHO WOULD BE DUMB ENOUGH TO ATTACK US?
I'VE FOUND THEM, MISTRESS MEDEA! WE'VE FINALLY CAUGHT UP TO SUNO AND HIS FRIENDS!
SOUNDS LIKE THEY'RE ON THEIR WAY OUT OF TOWN. HEADED TO THE FOREST OF SHADOWS.
WHAT A DELECTABLE DEVELOPMENT!
THERE'S ONLY ONE PATH THROUGH THAT FOREST, AND I KNOW IT LIKE THE BACK OF MY PERFECTLY MANICURED HAND! IT'S JUST THE PLACE TO CHALLENGE SUNO IN BATTLE.
AND KEEPING HIS MEDDLING FRIENDS OUT OF OUR BATTLE WILL BE A-
SNAP!
PACK IT UP, DARLINGS. WE'RE ON THE MOVE! WE'VE GOT TO BEAT SUNO AND HIS LITTLE FRIENDS TO THE FOREST.

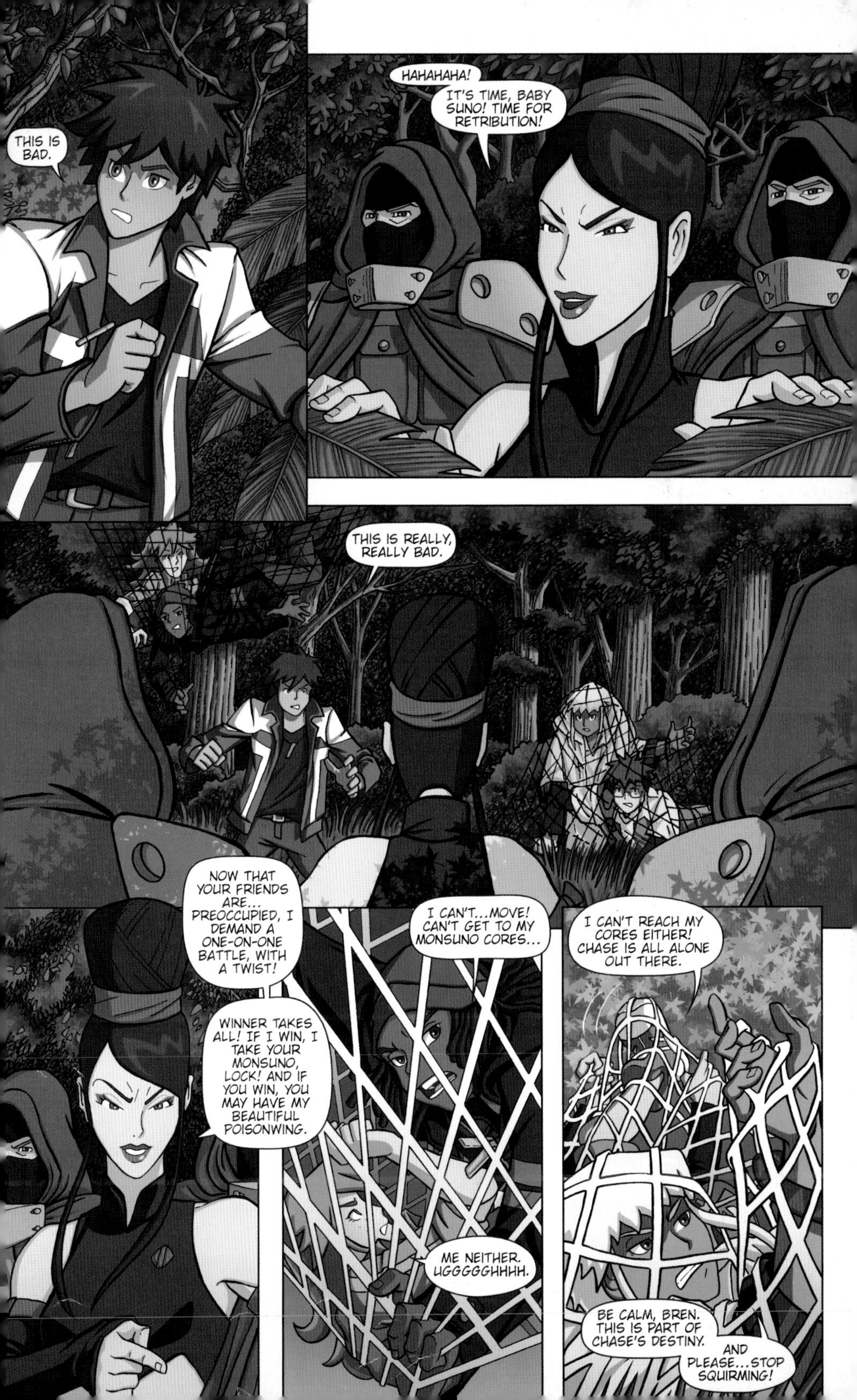
THIS IS BAD.
HAHAHAHA!
IT'S TIME, BABY SUNO! TIME FOR RETRIBUTION!
THIS IS REALLY, REALLY BAD.
NOW THAT YOUR FRIENDS ARE... PREOCCUPIED, I DEMAND A ONE-ON-ONE BATTLE, WITH A TWIST!
WINNER TAKES ALL! IF I WIN, I TAKE YOUR MONSUNO, LOCK! AND IF YOU WIN, YOU MAY HAVE MY BEAUTIFUL POISONWING.
I CAN'T...MOVE! CAN'T GET TO MY MONSUNO CORES...
ME NEITHER. UGGGGGHHHH.
I CAN'T REACH MY CORES EITHER! CHASE IS ALL ALONE OUT THERE.
BE CALM, BREN. THIS IS PART OF CHASE'S DESTINY.
AND PLEASE...STOP SQUIRMING!

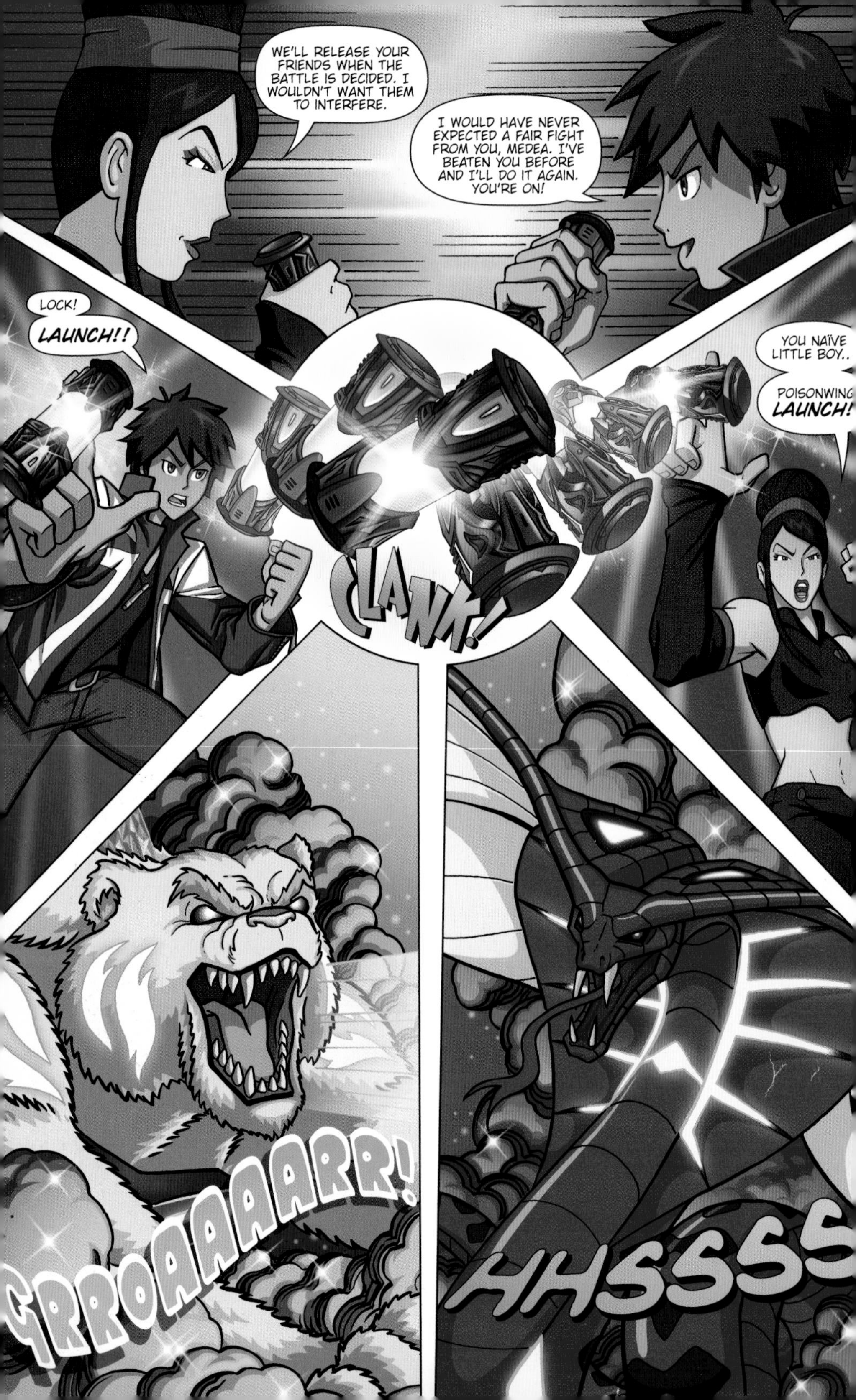
WE'LL RELEASE YOUR FRIENDS WHEN THE BATTLE IS DECIDED. I WOULDN'T WANT THEM TO INTERFERE.
I WOULD HAVE NEVER EXPECTED A FAIR FIGHT FROM YOU, MEDEA. I'VE BEATEN YOU BEFORE AND I'LL DO IT AGAIN. YOU'RE ON!
LOCK!
LAUNCH!!
YOU NAÏVE LITTLE BOY..
POISONWING LAUNCH!
CLANK!
GRROAAAAARR!
HHSSSSS

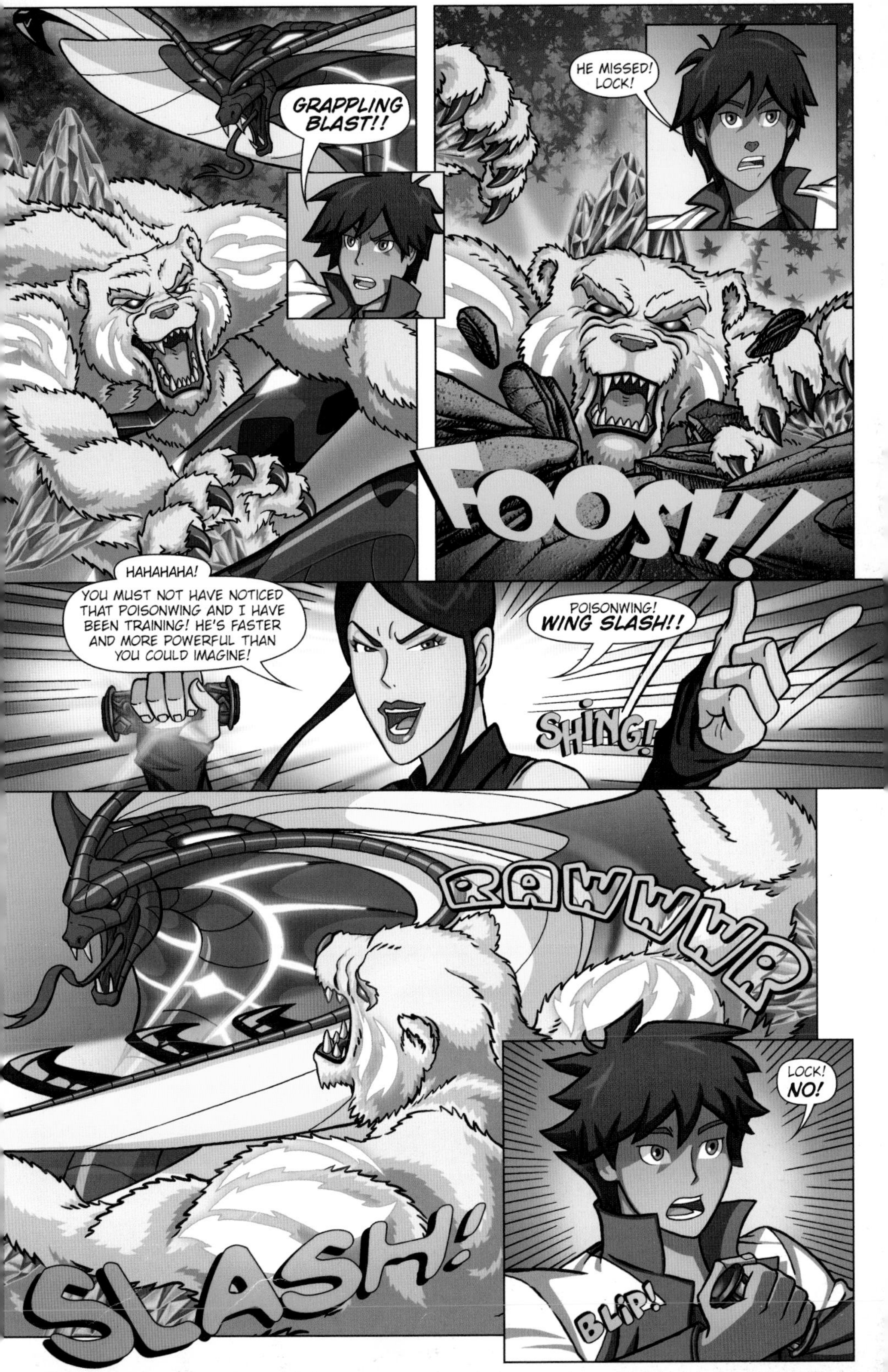
GRAPPLING BLAST!!
HE MISSED! LOCK!
FOOSH!
HAHAHAHA!
YOU MUST NOT HAVE NOTICED THAT POISONWING AND I HAVE BEEN TRAINING! HE'S FASTER AND MORE POWERFUL THAN YOU COULD IMAGINE!
POISONWING! WING SLASH!!
SHING!
RAWWWR
SLASH!
LOCK! NO!
BLIP!

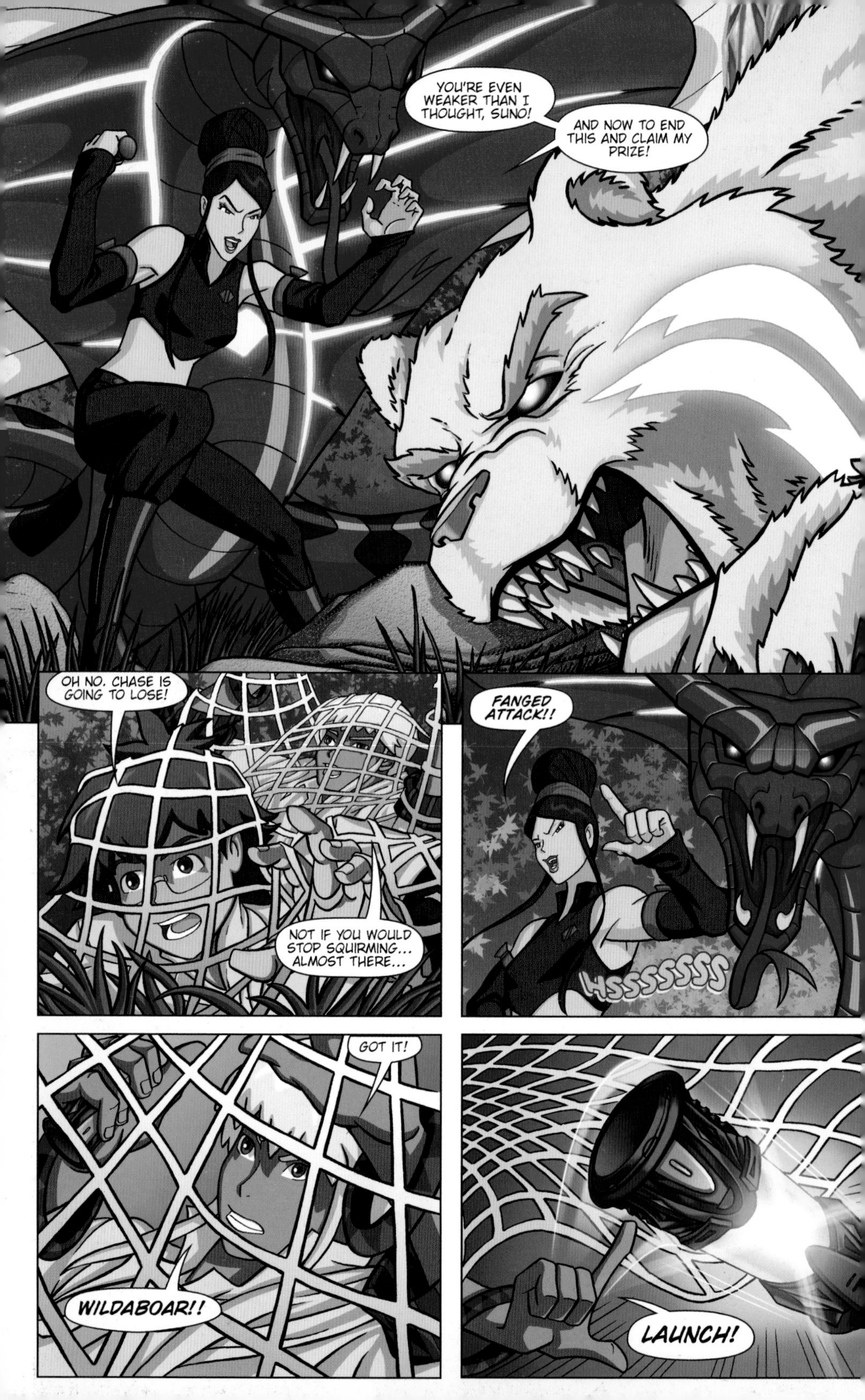
YOU'RE EVEN WEAKER THAN I THOUGHT, SUNO!
AND NOW TO END THIS AND CLAIM MY PRIZE!
OH NO. CHASE IS GOING TO LOSE!
NOT IF YOU WOULD STOP SQUIRMING... ALMOST THERE...
FANGED ATTACK!!
HSSSSSSS
GOT IT!
WILDABOAR!!
LAUNCH!

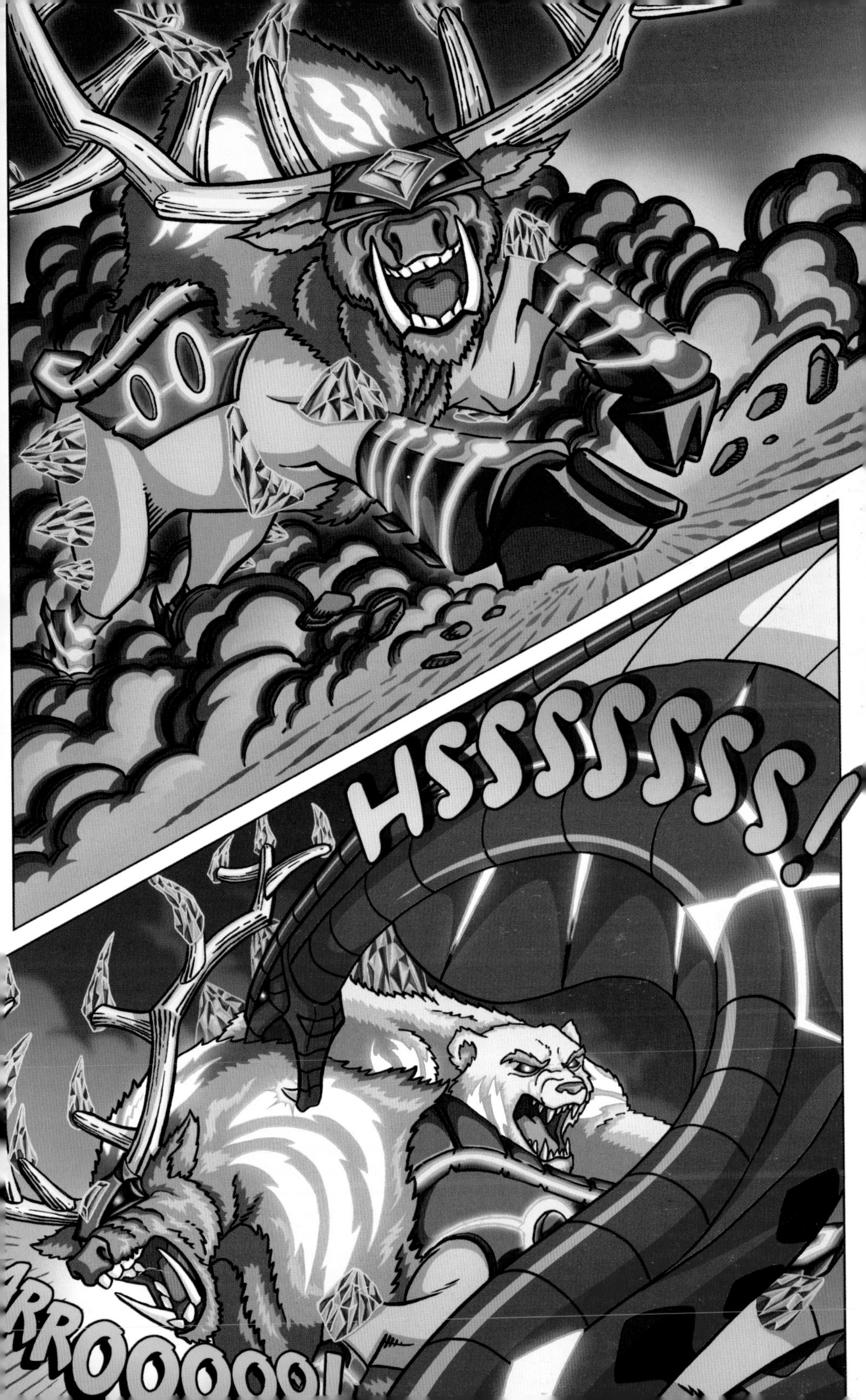
HSSSSSSS!!
RROOOOO!

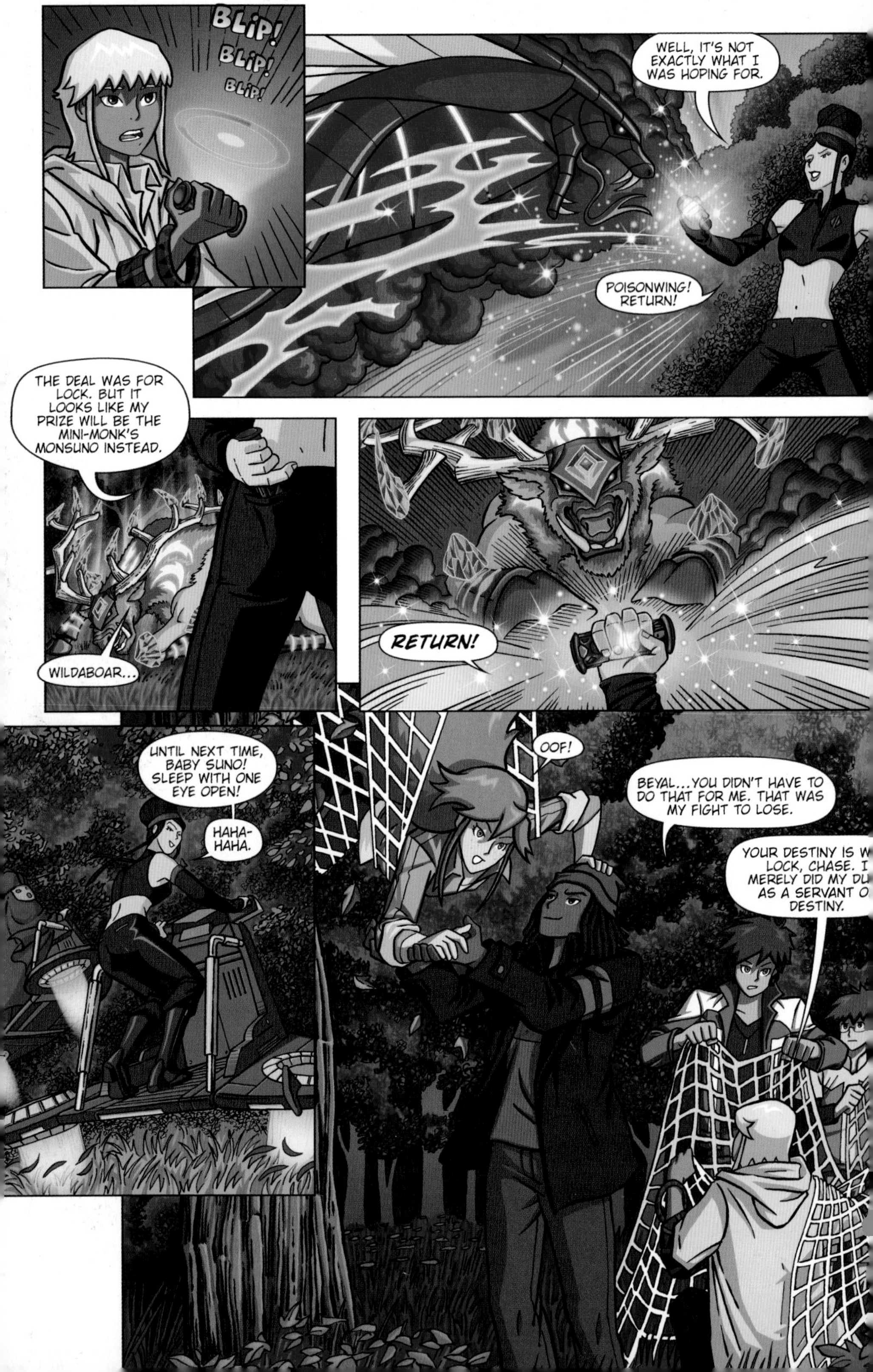
BLIP! BLIP! BLIP!
WELL, IT'S NOT EXACTLY WHAT I WAS HOPING FOR.
POISONWING! RETURN!
THE DEAL WAS FOR LOCK. BUT IT LOOKS LIKE MY PRIZE WILL BE THE MINI-MONK'S MONSUNO INSTEAD.
WILDABOAR...
RETURN!
UNTIL NEXT TIME, BABY SUNO! SLEEP WITH ONE EYE OPEN!
HAHA-HAHA.
OOF!
BEYAL...YOU DIDN'T HAVE TO DO THAT FOR ME. THAT WAS MY FIGHT TO LOSE.

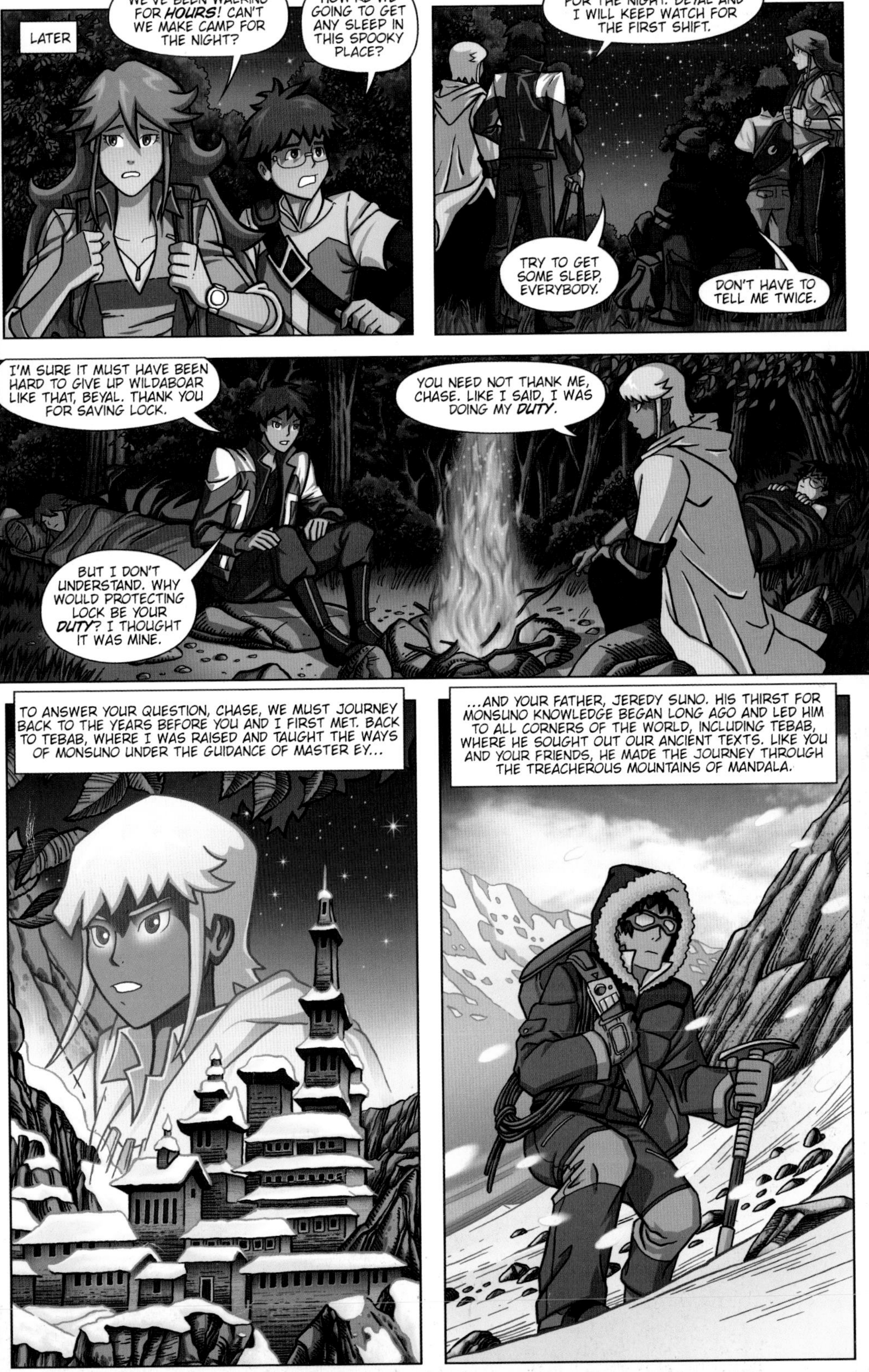
LATER
WE'VE BEEN WALKING FOR HOURS! CAN'T WE MAKE CAMP FOR THE NIGHT?
HOW'RE WE GOING TO GET ANY SLEEP IN THIS SPOOKY PLACE?
WE'LL BED DOWN HERE FOR THE NIGHT. BEYAL AND I WILL KEEP WATCH FOR THE FIRST SHIFT.
TRY TO GET SOME SLEEP, EVERYBODY.
DON'T HAVE TO TELL ME TWICE.
I'M SURE IT MUST HAVE BEEN HARD TO GIVE UP WILDABOAR LIKE THAT, BEYAL. THANK YOU FOR SAVING LOCK.
YOU NEED NOT THANK ME, CHASE. LIKE I SAID, I WAS DOING MY DUTY.
BUT I DON'T UNDERSTAND. WHY WOULD PROTECTING LOCK BE YOUR DUTY? I THOUGHT IT WAS MINE.
TO ANSWER YOUR QUESTION, CHASE, WE MUST JOURNEY BACK TO THE YEARS BEFORE YOU AND I FIRST MET. BACK TO TEBAB, WHERE I WAS RAISED AND TAUGHT THE WAYS OF MONSUNO UNDER THE GUIDANCE OF MASTER EY...
...AND YOUR FATHER, JEREDY SUNO. HIS THIRST FOR MONSUNO KNOWLEDGE BEGAN LONG AGO AND LED HIM TO ALL CORNERS OF THE WORLD, INCLUDING TEBAB, WHERE HE SOUGHT OUT OUR ANCIENT TEXTS. LIKE YOU AND YOUR FRIENDS, HE MADE THE JOURNEY THROUGH THE TREACHEROUS MOUNTAINS OF MANDALA.

DESPITE HIS COURAGE, FATE WOULD NOT AFFORD YOUR FATHER A PEACEFUL JOURNEY TO TEBAB. MOUNTAIN WEATHER CAN CHANGE SUDDENLY, AND WHEN A DANGEROUS STORM SURPRISED YOUR FATHER DURING HIS CLIMB, IT PREVENTED HIM FROM COMPLETING HIS JOURNEY.

THE STORM NEARLY TOOK HIS LIFE. BUT YOUR FATHER'S DESTINY WAS TO LIVE. HIS DESTINY, LIKE YOURS, IS SOMETHING GREATER.

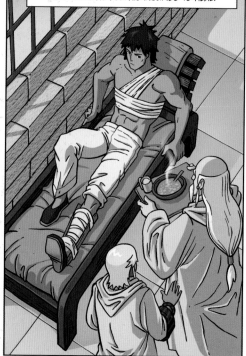

THE MONKS OF TEBAB FOUND JEREDY SUNO IN THE SNOW AND BROUGHT HIM TO THE MONASTERY. WE GAVE HIM THE BEST CARE WE COULD, BUT IT TOOK MANY MONTHS FOR HIS INJURIES TO HEAL.

DURING HIS RECOVERY, YOUR FATHER SPENT MANY HOURS IN OUR LIBRARY. HE STUDIED ANCIENT TEXTS FROM SUNRISE TO SUNDOWN. HIS INJURIES DID NOT DAMPEN HIS APPETITE FOR MONSUNO KNOWLEDGE.

EVEN THOUGH THE MONKS OF TEBAB STUDIED MONSUNO FOR GENERATIONS, THEY WERE A PEACEFUL ORDER AND DID NOT BELIEVE IN MONSUNO BATTLE. THE MONKS FOCUSED ON STRENGTHENING THE CONNECTION BETWEEN A MONSUNO AND ITS CONTROLLER. I HAD NEVER BEFORE SEEN SOMEONE COMMAND MONSUNO AS YOUR FATHER DID.

BUT WHEN THE BOOKMAN ARRIVED WITH HIS ARMY, HE SURPRISED US WITH HIS NUMBERS. THE MONKS OF MY ORDER WERE NOT PREPARED TO DO BATTLE, AND WE WERE OVERWHELMED. MANY LIVES WERE LOST.

DESPITE HIS INJURIES, YOUR FATHER FOUGHT VALIANTLY TO PROTECT US. HE CHALLENGED THE BOOKMAN TO BATTLE, BELIEVING THAT IF HE COULD DEFEAT HIM, BOOKMAN'S SOLDIERS WOULD RETREAT.

THE FORCE OF THEIR BATTLE CAUSED GREAT DAMAGE TO THE LIBRARY'S MAIN ATRIUM. THE STRUCTURE NEARLY COLLAPSED, BURYING CENTURIES OF KNOWLEDGE.

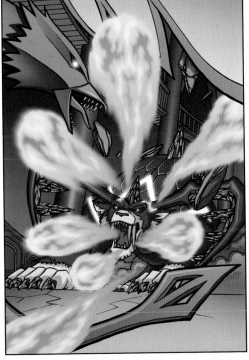

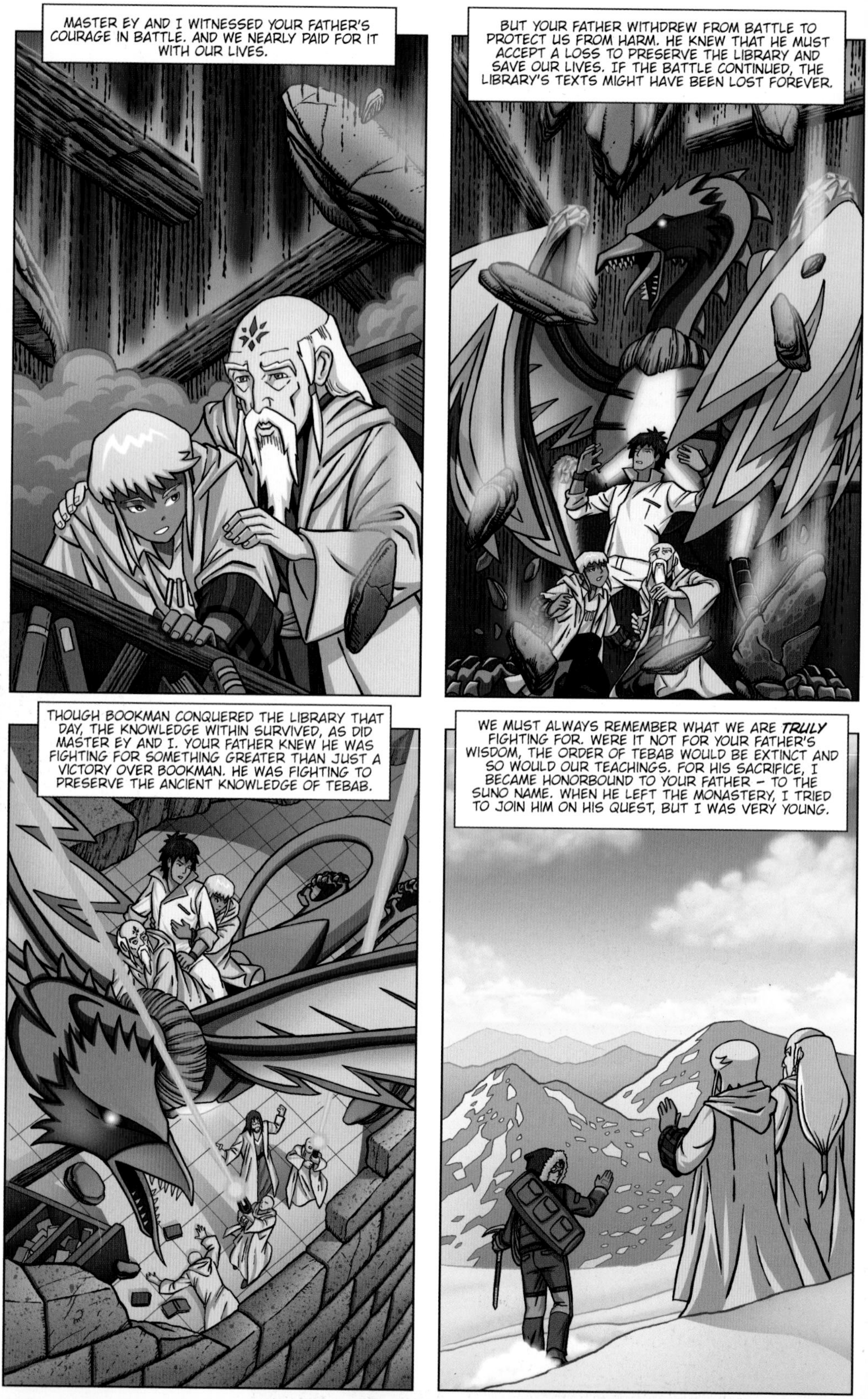
MASTER EY AND I WITNESSED YOUR FATHER'S COURAGE IN BATTLE. AND WE NEARLY PAID FOR IT WITH OUR LIVES.
BUT YOUR FATHER WITHDREW FROM BATTLE TO PROTECT US FROM HARM. HE KNEW THAT HE MUST ACCEPT A LOSS TO PRESERVE THE LIBRARY AND SAVE OUR LIVES. IF THE BATTLE CONTINUED, THE LIBRARY'S TEXTS MIGHT HAVE BEEN LOST FOREVER.
THOUGH BOOKMAN CONQUERED THE LIBRARY THAT DAY, THE KNOWLEDGE WITHIN SURVIVED, AS DID MASTER EY AND I. YOUR FATHER KNEW HE WAS FIGHTING FOR SOMETHING GREATER THAN JUST A VICTORY OVER BOOKMAN. HE WAS FIGHTING TO PRESERVE THE ANCIENT KNOWLEDGE OF TEBAB.
WE MUST ALWAYS REMEMBER WHAT WE ARE *TRULY* FIGHTING FOR. WERE IT NOT FOR YOUR FATHER'S WISDOM, THE ORDER OF TEBAB WOULD BE EXTINCT AND SO WOULD OUR TEACHINGS. FOR HIS SACRIFICE, I BECAME HONORBOUND TO YOUR FATHER – TO THE SUNO NAME. WHEN HE LEFT THE MONASTERY, I TRIED TO JOIN HIM ON HIS QUEST, BUT I WAS VERY YOUNG.

YEARS LATER, WHEN YOU AND YOUR FRIENDS CAME TO THE LIBRARY OF TEBAB, I KNEW OUR FATES WERE INTERTWINED. THE TIME FOR ME TO FULFILL MY DUTY TO THE SUNO NAME HAD COME.

MY DESTINY IS TO HELP YOU FULFILL YOURS, CHASE. THAT IS WHAT I FIGHT FOR.

SO THAT'S WHY YOU JOINED OUR TEAM?

IT IS.

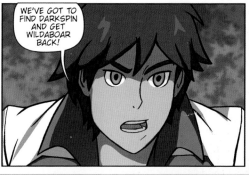

WE'VE GOT TO FIND DARKSPIN AND GET WILDABOAR BACK!

HOSE HOVERBOARDS DARKSPIN WAS SING LEFT A DISTINCT PATH, BUT THIS FOREST IS SO DENSE. IT'S REALLY OWING US DOWN, MATE. WE NEED TO VE FASTER IF WE HOPE TO CATCH UP.

ARE YOU SURE ABOUT THIS, CHASE? WE MIGHT MISS YOUR DAD. MAYBE WE SHOULD SPLIT UP.

OF COURSE I'M SURE. WE'RE A TEAM AND WE STICK *TOGETHER*.

BESIDES, I KNOW WHAT WILL SPEED THINGS UP!

NIGHTSTONE... *LAUNCH!!*

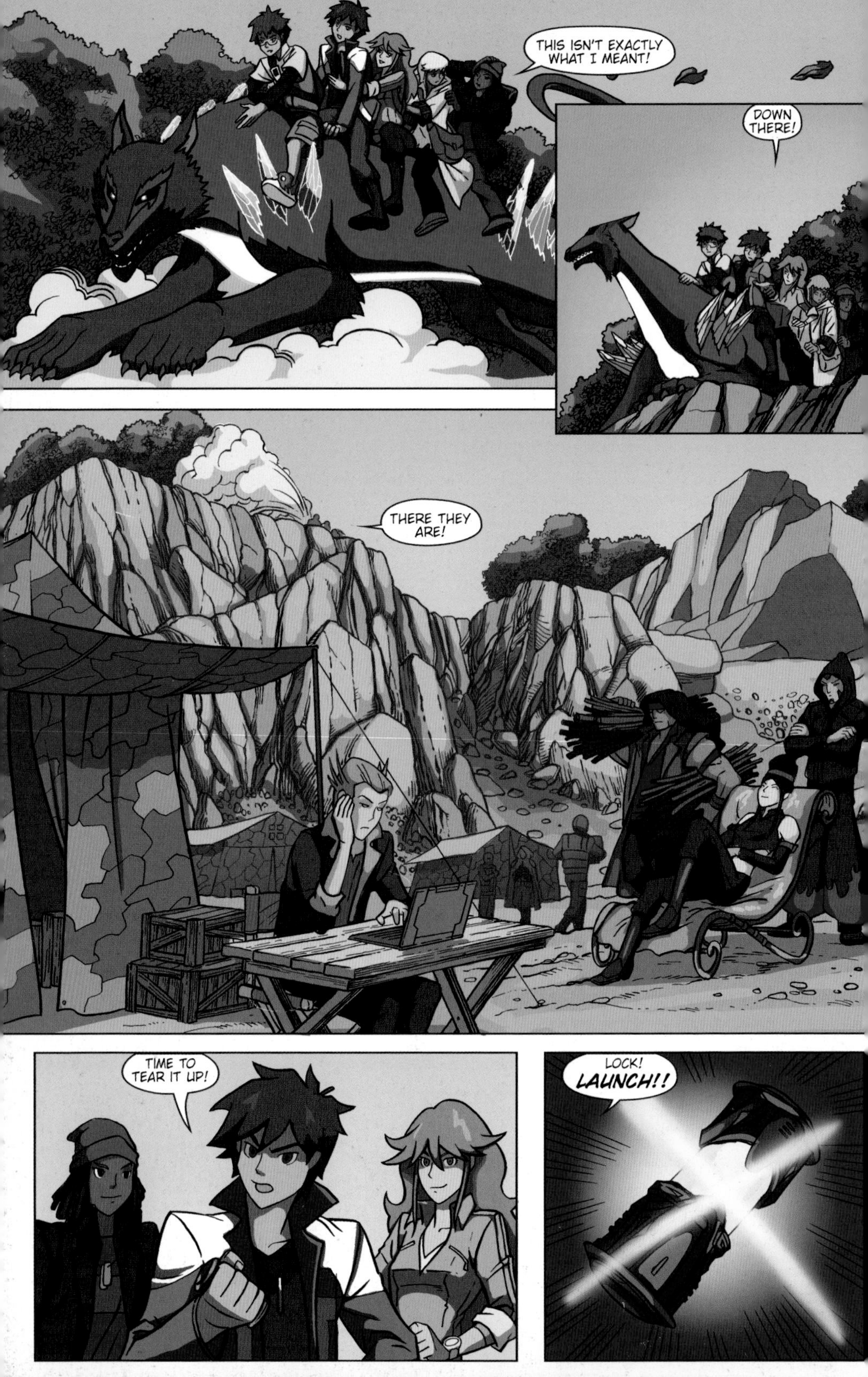
THIS ISN'T EXACTLY WHAT I MEANT!
DOWN THERE!
THERE THEY ARE!
TIME TO TEAR IT UP!
LOCK! **LAUNCH!!**

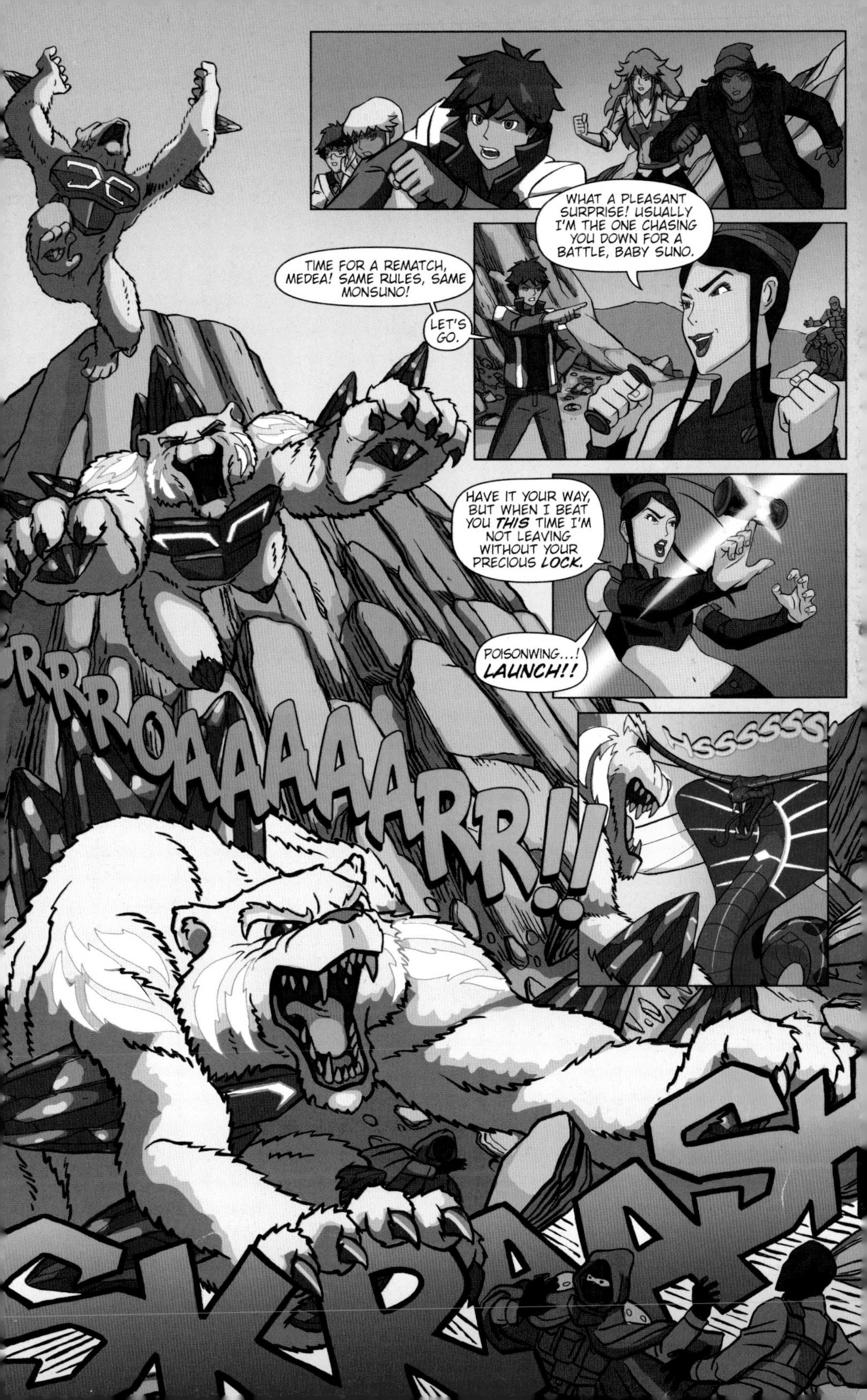
WHAT A PLEASANT SURPRISE! USUALLY I'M THE ONE CHASING YOU DOWN FOR A BATTLE, BABY SUNO.
TIME FOR A REMATCH, MEDEA! SAME RULES, SAME MONSUNO!
LET'S GO.
HAVE IT YOUR WAY, BUT WHEN I BEAT YOU THIS TIME I'M NOT LEAVING WITHOUT YOUR PRECIOUS LOCK.
POISONWING...! LAUNCH!!
RRRROAAAAAARR!!
HSSSSSS!

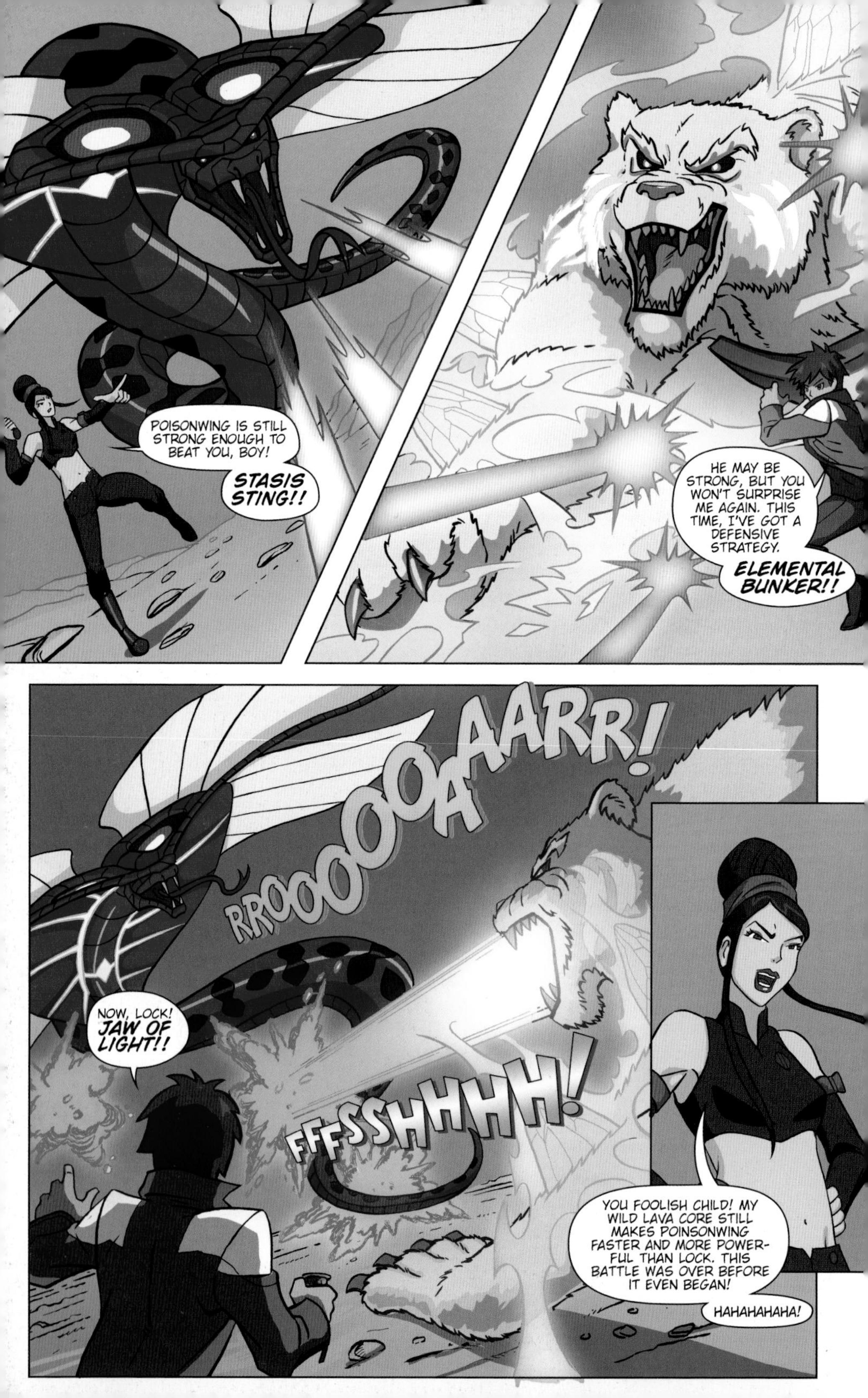
POISONWING IS STILL STRONG ENOUGH TO BEAT YOU, BOY!
STASIS STING!!
HE MAY BE STRONG, BUT YOU WON'T SURPRISE ME AGAIN. THIS TIME, I'VE GOT A DEFENSIVE STRATEGY.
ELEMENTAL BUNKER!!
RROOOOOOAAARR!
NOW, LOCK! JAW OF LIGHT!!
FFFSSHHHH!
YOU FOOLISH CHILD! MY WILD LAVA CORE STILL MAKES POINSONWING FASTER AND MORE POWER-FUL THAN LOCK. THIS BATTLE WAS OVER BEFORE IT EVEN BEGAN!
HAHAHAHAHA!

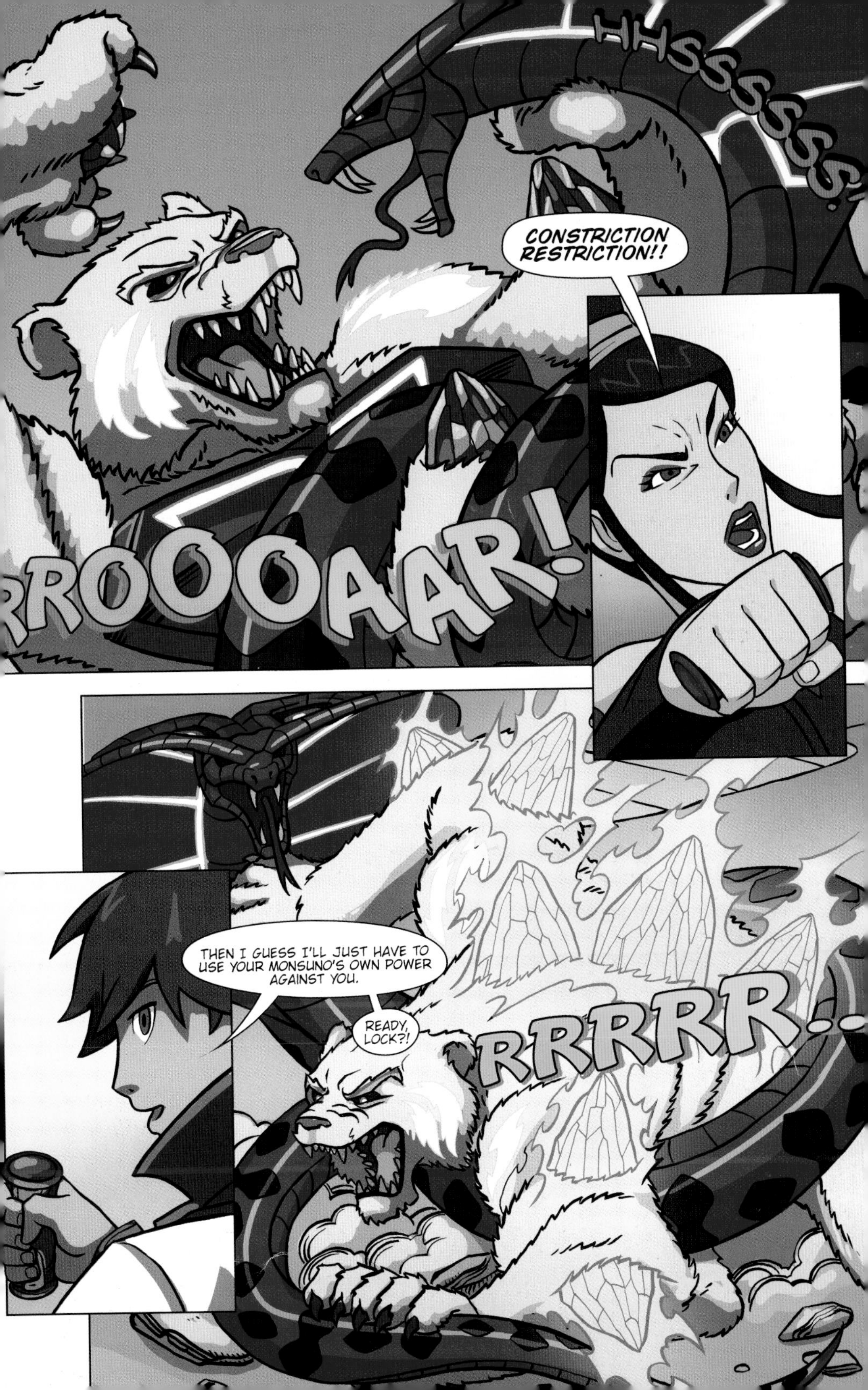
HHSSSSSS!
CONSTRICTION RESTRICTION!!
RROOOAAR!
THEN I GUESS I'LL JUST HAVE TO USE YOUR MONSUNO'S OWN POWER AGAINST YOU.
READY, LOCK?!
RRRRRR...

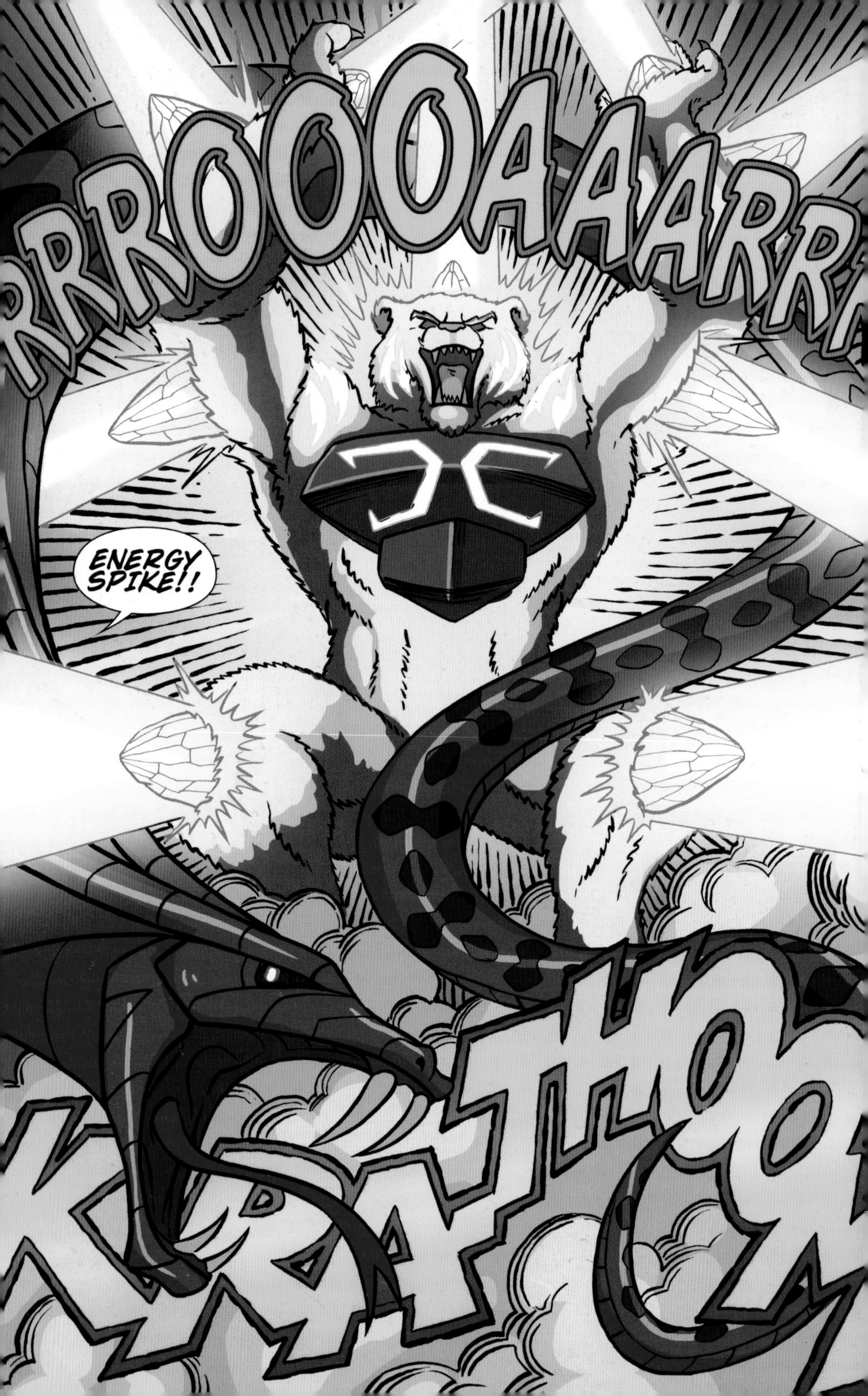
RROOOAAARR
ENERGY SPIKE!!

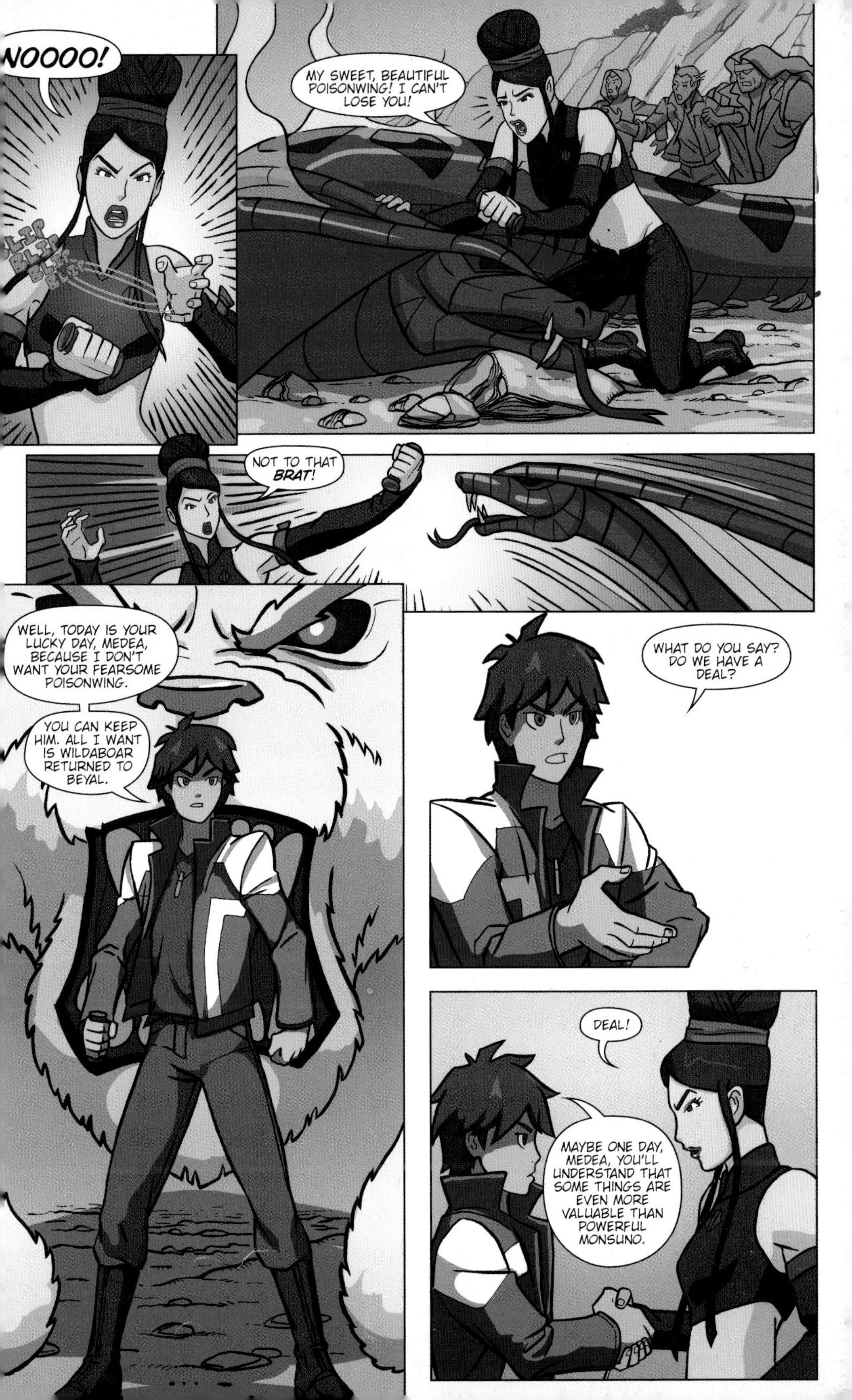
NOOOO!
BLIP BLIP BLIP BLIP
MY SWEET, BEAUTIFUL POISONWING! I CAN'T LOSE YOU!
NOT TO THAT *BRAT*!
WELL, TODAY IS YOUR LUCKY DAY, MEDEA, BECAUSE I DON'T WANT YOUR FEARSOME POISONWING.
YOU CAN KEEP HIM. ALL I WANT IS WILDABOAR RETURNED TO BEYAL.
WHAT DO YOU SAY? DO WE HAVE A DEAL?
DEAL!
MAYBE ONE DAY, MEDEA, YOU'LL UNDERSTAND THAT SOME THINGS ARE EVEN MORE VALUABLE THAN POWERFUL MONSUNO.

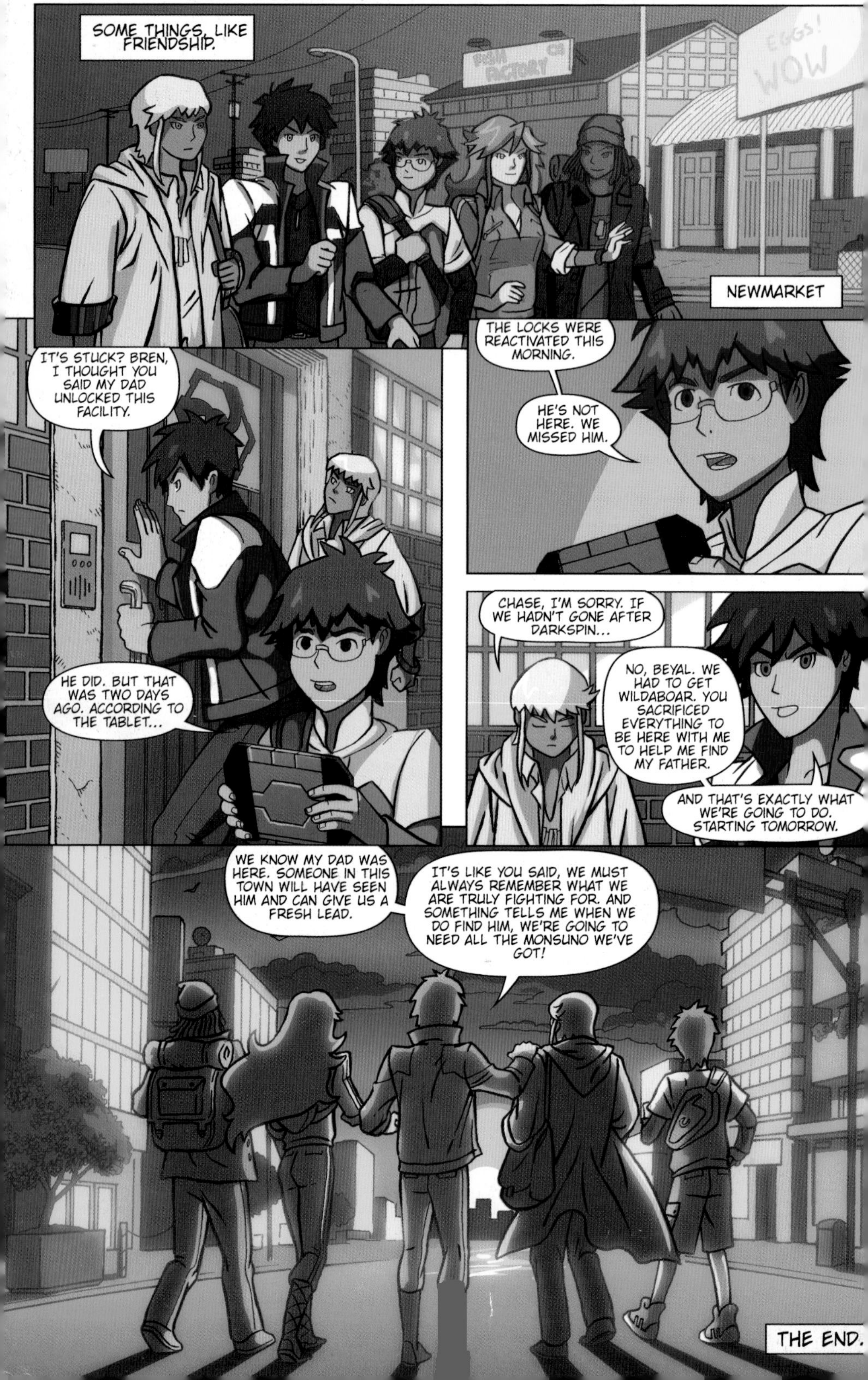
SOME THINGS, LIKE FRIENDSHIP.
FISH FACTORY
EGGS! WOW
NEWMARKET
IT'S STUCK? BREN, I THOUGHT YOU SAID MY DAD UNLOCKED THIS FACILITY.
HE DID. BUT THAT WAS TWO DAYS AGO. ACCORDING TO THE TABLET...
THE LOCKS WERE REACTIVATED THIS MORNING.
HE'S NOT HERE. WE MISSED HIM.
CHASE, I'M SORRY. IF WE HADN'T GONE AFTER DARKSPIN...
NO, BEYAL. WE HAD TO GET WILDABOAR. YOU SACRIFICED EVERYTHING TO BE HERE WITH ME TO HELP ME FIND MY FATHER.
AND THAT'S EXACTLY WHAT WE'RE GOING TO DO. STARTING TOMORROW.
WE KNOW MY DAD WAS HERE. SOMEONE IN THIS TOWN WILL HAVE SEEN HIM AND CAN GIVE US A FRESH LEAD.
IT'S LIKE YOU SAID, WE MUST ALWAYS REMEMBER WHAT WE ARE TRULY FIGHTING FOR. AND SOMETHING TELLS ME WHEN WE DO FIND HIM, WE'RE GOING TO NEED ALL THE MONSUNO WE'VE GOT!
THE END.

WRITERS

BRIAN SMITH is a former Marvel Comics editor. His credits include *The Ultimates*, *Ultimate Spider-Man*, *Iron Man*, *Captain America*, *The Incredible Hulk* and dozens of other comics. Smith is the co-creator/writer behind the *New York Times* best-selling graphic novel *The Stuff of Legend*, and the writer/artist of all-ages comic *The Intrepid EscapeGoat*. His writing credits include *Finding Nemo: Losing Dory* from BOOM! Studios, and *SpongeBob Comics* from Bongo.

CORY LEVINE is a former editorial staffer for Marvel Comics where he edited hundreds of collected editions of comic books, encyclopedic handbooks, special edition magazines and foreign-licensed comics, including the company's well-received line of Soleil graphic album adaptations. In 2010 he founded First Edition Publishing, Inc., an end-to-end publishing solutions firm offering editorial packaging, graphic design and pre-press production services.

ARTISTS

PAPILLON STUDIOS is a full-production house run out of Indonesia by artist ALFA ROBBI, who has illustrated *Voltron Force: Rise of the Beast King* for VIZ as well as *Planetary Brigade* (TokyoPop), and FAJAR BUANA, a colorist and illustrator who has worked for Arcana. Other team members include ERWIN PRASETYA, who drew this comic; ANGGA PRASETYAWAN, who assisted with additional art; inker ARUM SETIADI; and inker and colorist FANDHI GILANG WIJANARKO, who also inked *Voltron Force: Rise of the Beast King* for VIZ.

MAURIZIO CAMPIDELLI lives and works in Rimini, Italy, mainly as an illustrator, in collaboration with advertising agencies and publishers. His particular style has resulted in his art being exhibited in Italy, Paris and Taiwan.

LETTERER/COLORIST

ZACK TURNER started out in the comics industry as an independent artist and colorist who worked on *Unimaginable* (Arcana) and several projects for Bluewater. Recently he has been working on full art duties on *Redakai* (VIZ Media).

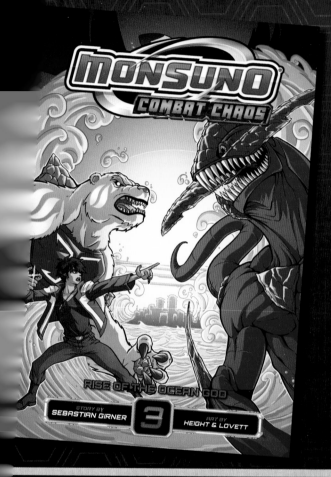

MONSUNO
COMBAT CHAOS

RISE OF THE OCEAN GOD

STORY BY
SEBASTIAN GIRNER

3

ART BY
HEIGHT & LOVETT

Bren, Jinja and the others travel to a faraway
to find the mysterious Dr. Serizawa, who may have
ation about Chase's missing dad. Instead, they come
-face with an old enemy and an ancient secret that
s everything they think they know about the history of
no on Earth...and puts the entire world in peril!

t in volume 3 of MONSUNO: RISE OF THE OCEAN GOD

le December 2013!